~ • ~

BRYNN THORNWICK:

Guardian of the Crimson Crown

~ • ~

by

Jackie L. Smith

Copyright Page

Brynn Thornwick: *Guardian of the Crimson Crown*

Dedication

For the boys who played in Kentucky caves,

believed in magic,

and never stopped seeking adventures.

This one's for us.

Also by Jackie L. Smith

Table of Contents

Chapter 1: The Map's Discovery

The morning sun filtered through the wooden slats of her grandmother's attic, each golden beam catching dust motes that drifted through the still air like miniature stars suspended in amber light. Brynn Thornwick: pulled herself up through the narrow opening in the ceiling, her hands gripping the rough-hewn edge of the trapdoor as she heaved her body into the cramped space above. The ladder creaked beneath her weight—old wood protesting against use after months, perhaps years, of neglect.

Her heart hammered against her ribs, though whether from exertion or anticipation, she couldn't say. Probably both.

The attic smelled of time itself—old wood and dried lavender, mothballs and ancient paper, the peculiar mustiness that only comes from things long forgotten. Cobwebs draped across the rafters like lacework made by patient, invisible hands. Trunks and boxes stood stacked in precarious towers against the sloped walls, each one labeled in her grandmother's precise, flowing script: *Household Linens. Good China—Handle Carefully. Family Portraits—Keep Safe.*

Brynn had explored every inch of Grandmother Meredith's cottage over the past fortnight since the funeral. The kitchen with its bundles of dried herbs hanging from hooks, their scents still potent even in death. The parlor with its faded photographs in tarnished silver frames—her grandmother as a young woman, beautiful and fierce-eyed, standing beside a man Brynn had never met. The garden where roses still bloomed as if mourning, their petals dropping like crimson tears onto the overgrown grass.

Yet the attic had remained locked until this morning, when Brynn had discovered the key hanging on a nail behind the kitchen door, partially hidden by an embroidered tea towel. The key itself was unusual—brass, ornate, with a strange symbol etched into its handle that looked almost like a crown.

Strange, Brynn thought, turning it over in her palm before climbing the ladder. *I've never noticed this before.*

Now, standing in the attic's dusty gloom, she wondered what secrets her grandmother had kept locked away up here. Aubre Thornwick had been a woman of mysteries—kind and gentle on the surface, but with depths Brynn had only glimpsed in stories told by firelight on winter evenings. Stories of ancient kings and forgotten magic, of quests undertaken and prices paid.

"Just stories," Brynn's mother had always said dismissively. "Your grandmother had an active imagination. Don't take them seriously."

But Brynn had taken them seriously. Even as a child, she'd sensed truth buried beneath the fantasy, the way one senses bone beneath flesh. And now, with her grandmother gone, those stories felt more important than ever—as if they were all she had left of the woman who had raised her after her own mother had...

Brynn shook her head, banishing that thought. This wasn't the time for old grief.

She moved carefully through the cluttered space, her boots stirring up clouds of dust with each step. The floorboards creaked alarmingly, and she made a mental note to step only on the joists if possible. Morning light slanted through gaps in the roof tiles, creating dramatic columns of illumination that made the attic feel almost cathedral-like in its atmosphere.

Most of the boxes contained exactly what their labels promised—linens, dishes, old curtains saved for some future purpose that never came. But as Brynn worked her way deeper into the space, she found containers that were unmarked, or marked only with symbols she didn't recognize.

And then she saw it.

In the far corner, tucked beneath an ancient quilt that might have been beautiful once, sat a trunk unlike the others. It was darker, made of wood that seemed to absorb light rather than reflect it. Iron bands reinforced its corners, and the lock was an elaborate affair of brass and crystal that gleamed despite decades of neglect.

Brynn approached it slowly, her breath coming faster. This was it—whatever her grandmother had wanted kept secret, it was in this trunk. She could feel it the way she'd felt things all her life, that peculiar certainty that some called intuition and others called foolishness.

The lock should have required a key, but when Brynn touched it, the mechanism clicked open with a sound like a sigh of relief. As if it had been waiting for her.

That's ridiculous, she told herself, even as goose bumps prickled along her arms. *Locks don't wait for people.*

She lifted the heavy lid, hinges protesting with a squeal of disused metal. Inside, nestled in folds of midnight-blue velvet, lay treasures that made her gasp aloud.

Scrolls tied with ribbon—some looked ancient, their parchment yellowed and brittle, covered in languages she didn't recognize. Letters in sealed envelopes addressed in her grandmother's hand but never sent. A small wooden box containing what appeared to be dried flowers, though their colors remained impossibly vivid. A leather journal with a lock of its own.

And beneath it all, rolled and tied with a cord of braided silver, was a map.

Brynn's hands trembled as she lifted it from the trunk. The parchment felt warm to the touch—not uncomfortably so, but distinctly warmer than it should be given the chill of the attic. It was heavier than expected, too, as if it carried weight beyond the physical.

She moved to a shaft of sunlight and carefully untied the cord. It slithered away like something alive, coiling on the floor beside her. The map unfurled with a whisper of sound, and Brynn's breath caught in her throat.

It was beautiful.

The parchment itself was cream-colored and flawless, no sign of age despite what must be considerable years. The illustrations were exquisite, rendered in inks that seemed to shimmer and shift in the light—deep blue's for rivers, emerald greens for forests, browns and grays for mountains that looked sharp enough to cut.

At first, she recognized the landmarks. There was Thornhaven, her village, rendered in perfect detail down to the specific placement of buildings and streets. She could see the market square, the church with its distinctive bell tower, even the forge where Thomas worked, marked with a tiny hammer symbol.

But beyond Thornhaven's borders, the map showed things that shouldn't exist.

Mountains shaped like fangs, their peaks sharp and threatening, rising from terrain that in reality was nothing but gentle hills. Rivers that flowed with what appeared to be liquid silver, their courses winding through forests rendered in gold ink rather than green. Castles that seemed to float in midair. Creatures drawn in the margins—some beautiful, some terrifying, all impossible.

And at the very center of the map, marked with a symbol that pulsed with its own inner light, was a location labeled in ornate script: The Crimson Crown.

The symbol itself was extraordinary—a crown rendered in what looked like actual rubies embedded in the parchment, surrounded by a circle of text in a language that hurt to look at directly, as if the letters themselves resisted being read.

Brynn reached out, unable to stop herself, and touched one fingertip to the crown symbol.

Heat shot up her arm like lightning made of fire and music combined. She gasped, trying to pull away, but found herself frozen, her finger pressed to the parchment as sensation flooded through her.

Visions.

She saw a smithy, but not Thomas's familiar forge—this was something grander, built of materials that gleamed like starlight. Figures worked there, tall and luminous, shaping reality itself with hammer and will. They were forging a crown, pouring into it power and purpose, binding it with oaths older than language.

The Crimson Crown, a voice whispered—though whether it spoke in her mind or the attic around her, she couldn't tell. *Forged in the First Age when magic flowed through the world like water through stone. Made to bridge realms, to balance light and shadow, to choose its guardian from among those pure of heart.*

The vision shifted. She saw battles—not the crude affairs of sword and shield, but conflicts where reality itself was the battlefield. Saw guardians wearing the crown, wielding power beyond imagining, protecting the balance between worlds.

Saw her grandmother.

Young, fierce, beautiful Aubre standing in a room Brynn didn't recognize, the map spread before her just as it was spread before Brynn now. Her grandmother's finger touched the crown symbol,

and the same heat, the same visions, flowed through
her.

But she never claimed it, Brynn realized. *She
never went on the quest. Why?*

The answer came with the force of certainty:
*She was waiting. Waiting to pass it to the next
guardian. Waiting for me.*

The visions released her abruptly. Brynn
stumbled backward, gasping, her heart racing. The
attic around her seemed more real than it had
moments before, colors brighter, edges sharper, as
if she'd been living in a faded copy of the world and
had suddenly been shown the original.

She looked down at the map, still glowing
faintly in her hands. The crown symbol pulsed like a
heartbeat.

"This is real," she whispered to the empty
attic. "It's actually real."

Her grandmother's stories flooded back—tales
told by firelight while wind howled outside and tea
grew cold in forgotten cups. Stories of the Crimson
Crown and its guardians, of the Celestial Smiths
who had forged it, of the balance that must be

maintained between light and shadow or else the world itself would tear apart.

The crown chooses its guardian, her grandmother had said, leaning close with eyes that reflected firelight like molten gold. *Not for power or nobility, but for heart. For the capacity to hold mercy and justice in the same hand, to be strong enough to protect but wise enough to know when protection becomes tyranny.*

"But I'm not—" Brynn started to say aloud, then stopped.

Wasn't she? Hadn't she always felt different, set apart, as if she was meant for something more than the life Thornhaven offered? Hadn't she dreamed of adventure, of purpose, of a world larger than the one she could see from her bedroom window?

And hadn't her grandmother been preparing her all along, with those stories, with the way she'd taught Brynn to think and question and never accept easy answers?

Oh, Grandmother, Brynn thought, tears pricking her eyes. *Is this what you wanted? Is this why you never went yourself—because you were saving the quest for me?*

The map seemed to pulse in response, warm and alive in her hands.

Brynn made her decision in that moment, standing in dusty sunlight in her dead grandmother's attic. She would follow this map. She would seek the Crimson Crown. Not because she was certain she was worthy—she wasn't certain of anything—but because not trying felt like betraying everything her grandmother had been.

But she couldn't do it alone.

Brynn carefully rolled the map, noting how it seemed to roll itself, as if eager to be on the move. She tucked it inside her jacket, feeling its warmth against her ribs like a second heartbeat. Then she gathered the other treasures from the trunk—the journal, the letters, the scrolls—and carefully descended the ladder.

She had to find Thomas.

The forge was exactly where it had been for three generations of Blackwoods—on the eastern edge of Thornhaven, close enough to the village for convenience but far enough that the constant ring of hammer on anvil didn't disturb the peace. Smoke rose from the chimney in a steady stream, and even from a distance, Brynn could hear the familiar rhythm of Thomas at work.

Clang. Clang. Clang. Pause. Clang. Clang.

She found him bent over the anvil, stripped to his shirtsleeves despite the autumn chill, sweat gleaming on his forearms as he shaped what looked like a horseshoe. His dark hair was tied back with a leather cord, and his face held that expression of intense concentration he always wore when working —as if the entire world had narrowed to the piece of metal under his hammer and nothing else mattered.

It was one of the things she'd always admired about Thomas. His ability to focus, to commit fully to whatever task lay before him. Unlike her, he never seemed torn between what was and what might be. He was solid, grounded, real.

Which was exactly why she needed him for this impossible thing she was about to propose.

"Thomas!" she called, her voice barely audible over the ringing metal.

He looked up, startled, then smiled when he saw her. "Brynn! I wasn't expecting—" He paused, taking in her expression. His smile faded. "What's wrong?"

"Nothing's wrong. Or everything's wrong. Or nothing's wrong but everything's about to change." She realized she was babbling and forced herself to stop, take a breath. "I need to show you something."

Thomas set down his hammer and wiped his hands on a rag hanging from his belt. "Alright. Should I be worried?"

"I don't know. Maybe. Probably." Brynn looked around the forge—Thomas's apprentice was working at the bellows, and his father was visible through the office window, bent over account books. "Is there somewhere we can talk privately?"

Understanding flickered in Thomas's eyes. He'd known her long enough to recognize when something significant was happening. "Garden shed. No one will bother us there."

The shed was a small wooden structure behind the forge, used for storing charcoal and tools. It smelled of coal dust and leather oil, and the single window provided just enough light to see by. Thomas shut the door behind them and turned to face her.

"Alright," he said. "What's this about?"

Instead of answering, Brynn pulled the map from inside her jacket and spread it on the workbench that ran along one wall. Even in the shed's dim light, it seemed to glow, the illustrated features impossibly vivid.

Thomas leaned closer, his eyes widening. "That's... is that Thornhaven? But the rest of this—" He stopped, seeming at a loss for words.

"It's real," Brynn said quietly. "I found it in my grandmother's attic. Along with other things— journals, letters. Thomas, all those stories she used to tell us weren't just stories. They were history. Her history. And now..." She swallowed hard. "Now I think they're meant to be my history too."

Thomas was silent for a long moment, studying the map. His expression was unreadable— the same focused look he wore when examining a piece of metal, trying to determine its composition and quality.

"Touch it," Brynn said. "The crown symbol. Touch it and tell me what you feel."

He hesitated, then reached out and placed his fingertip on the glowing red crown at the map's center.

Brynn watched his eyes go distant, watched his breath catch. She couldn't see what visions the map was showing him, but she could see their effect—wonder and fear and something that might have been recognition flickering across his face.

When he pulled his hand away, his expression had changed. The skepticism that usually colored his view of anything fantastical was gone, replaced by something that looked almost like reverence.

"I heard music," he whispered. "And I saw... I don't even know how to describe it. Forges, but not like any forge I've ever seen. Smiths working with materials that don't exist. Creating something that wasn't just metal but..." He shook his head. "Magic. They were creating magic."

"The Celestial Smiths," Brynn said. "The ones who forged the crown. My grandmother told us about them, remember?"

"I thought it was a fairy tale."

"So did I. Until about an hour ago." Brynn leaned against the workbench. "Thomas, I have to follow this map. I have to find the crown. I don't completely understand why, but I know it's what my grandmother wanted. What she prepared me for. And I can't do it alone."

Thomas looked at her, then at the map, then back at her. "You're asking me to come with you."

"I'm asking you to help me do something that's probably impossible and definitely dangerous, that will take us away from everything we know, that might kill us or might change us so completely we can never come back to the lives we had before." She met his eyes. "So yes. I'm asking you to come with me."

He was quiet for so long that Brynn began to fear his answer. Thomas was practical, sensible, rooted in the real world of forge and anvil. Why would he leave all that for a quest that might be nothing more than an elaborate fantasy?

Finally, he spoke. "When do we leave?"

Relief flooded through her. "You'll come? Really?"

"Someone has to keep you from getting killed," he said with a slight smile. "And besides, I touched that map. I felt what it offered. I saw..." He paused, searching for words. "Purpose. Like everything I've done until now has been preparation for something larger. Does that sound insane?"

"No," Brynn said softly. "It sounds exactly right."

"Then we leave at dawn," Thomas said, his voice growing firmer as he made the decision. "That gives us today to prepare. I'll need to tell my father something—not the truth, he'd never believe it, but something plausible. And we'll need supplies, weapons, traveling gear."

"I'll gather what I can from my grandmother's house," Brynn said. "She left me money, and there are things in the attic that might be useful. Scrolls, books, a journal I haven't read yet."

They stood looking at each other across the glowing map, two childhood friends about to embark on something neither of them fully understood. Brynn felt fear and excitement warring in her chest, each emotion so powerful it was hard to tell them apart.

"Thank you," she said quietly. "For believing me. For coming with me."

"Always," Thomas replied. "Since we were children, right? When you decided we should climb to the top of Miller's windmill, and when you convinced me that jumping into the river from the high rocks was a good idea, and when you—"

"Got us both grounded for a week by 'borrowing' the mayor's horse?" Brynn finished with a laugh. "I remember. You've been following me into trouble since we were eight years old."

"And you've been leading me into adventures since the same age. Why stop now?" Thomas rolled up the map carefully and handed it back to her. "Go. Gather what you need. I'll do the same. We'll meet at the north edge of the village at dawn. And Brynn?"

"Yes?"

"Whatever this is, whatever we're walking into —I trust you. And I trust your grandmother's judgment in leaving this to you."

As Brynn walked back through Thornhaven's familiar streets, the map warm against her ribs and her heart full of purpose for the first time since her grandmother's death, she felt the world shifting around her. The ordinary becoming extraordinary. The impossible becoming real.

Tomorrow, her life would change forever.

Tonight, she had to prepare.

Chapter 2: Crossing The Threshold

Dawn broke over Thornhaven in shades of amber and rose, the sky painted in watercolor strokes that seemed almost too beautiful to be real. Brynn stood at the northern edge of the village, where cultivated fields gave way to wild forest, her pack settled on her shoulders with a weight that was both physical and metaphorical. She was carrying supplies, yes—food, water, a bedroll, her grandmother's journals—but also hope and fear in equal measure, uncertainty and determination braided together so tightly she couldn't separate one from the other.

The pack had taken her hours to prepare. She'd gone through her grandmother's house systematically, choosing items that might prove useful: a sturdy knife with a carved wooden handle, a flint and steel for making fire, a coil of rope that looked deceptively strong despite its age. From the attic trunk, she'd taken the leather journal—its small brass lock had clicked open when she touched it, just like the trunk itself—and several of the scrolls that bore symbols matching those on the map.

She'd also taken money. Her grandmother had left her a modest inheritance, not enough to live on forever but sufficient for a journey. Brynn had converted most of it to coin, which now weighed heavy in a purse at her belt. The rest she'd left with the village banker, with instructions that if she didn't return within three months, it should be donated to the church for charity.

Three months. The timeframe felt both impossibly long and frighteningly short. When she thought about it plainly, it sounded absolutely insane: three months to find an ancient artifact that might not exist, in lands that weren't on any real map, following directions that came from visions induced by touching magical parchment.

"Second thoughts?" a voice asked behind her.

Brynn turned to see Thomas emerging from the pre-dawn gloom, his own pack slung across broad shoulders that had been shaped by years of forge work. He wore practical traveling clothes—sturdy boots, thick trousers, a shirt and vest that would stand up to rough use. At his side hung a sword, newly forged, its scabbard still smelling of fresh leather and oil.

"You made that last night?" Brynn asked, gesturing to the weapon.

"Couldn't sleep anyway," Thomas said. "Figured I might as well make something useful." He rested his hand on the pommel. "It's not fancy, but it's well-balanced and the steel is good. Should serve if we need it."

"I hope we don't," Brynn said.

"So do I. But hope isn't a plan." Thomas looked past her at the forest, his jaw set in that determined way she recognized. He was nervous—she could see it in the tension of his shoulders, the way his hand kept drifting to the sword—but he'd made his choice and wouldn't back down now.

"Did you tell your father?" Brynn asked.

"Told him I was taking a commission to the eastern settlements," Thomas said. "Delivering a set of tools to a master smith who'd ordered them specially." His expression clouded with guilt. "I left a letter, like we discussed. If we're not back in three months, he'll open it and know the truth. Or at least, he'll know what we intended. Whether he believes it..." He shrugged helplessly.

"Then let's not waste daylight," Brynn said, pulling out the map. Even in the dim pre-dawn light, it seemed to glow faintly, the Crimson Crown symbol pulsing with its own inner radiance. "According to this, we head northeast toward the Misty Mountains. The first way marker should be somewhere in the foothills."

Thomas stepped closer, studying the map over her shoulder. "What kind of way marker?"

"The journal mentions an ancient altar," Brynn said. "That's all I know so far."

"Then let's find it," Thomas said.

With a deep breath that felt like inhaling possibility itself, Brynn stepped forward, crossing the invisible boundary between Thornhaven's cultivated fields and the wild forest beyond. Thomas fell into step beside her, and together they entered the ancient woods.

The forest embraced them immediately. Within a dozen steps, the village behind them had vanished, swallowed by trees and morning mist. The sounds changed too—no more distant roosters or creaking wagon wheels, just birdsong and the whisper of wind through leaves and the soft crunch of their boots on the forest floor.

"It's different here," Thomas said quietly after they'd been walking for perhaps twenty minutes.

"More real," Brynn agreed. "Like Thornhaven was somehow muted and this forest is showing us what the world actually looks like."

The trees here were old beyond memory, their trunks thick as houses, their canopy so dense that even the morning sun struggled to penetrate. But scattered rays still found their way through, creating dramatic columns of light that illuminated patches of wildflowers and moss-covered stones.

As they walked, Brynn found herself noticing details she would have missed in her normal life: the way spider webs caught light like jeweled necklaces, the spiral patterns in tree bark that seemed almost like writing, mushrooms growing in perfect circles that her grandmother had always warned her never to step inside.

"Do you feel it?" Brynn asked after they'd been walking perhaps an hour.

"Feel what?" Thomas replied.

"Like we're being watched," Brynn said. "But not threateningly. More like being... evaluated. As if the forest itself is taking our measure."

Thomas was quiet for a moment, then nodded. "I feel something. Like the forest is deciding whether we're worthy of passage."

They consulted the map periodically, confirming their direction against landmarks both natural and ancient. Around midday they stopped beside a brook that ran clear and cold over smooth stones. The water tasted impossibly pure, so cold it made Brynn's teeth ache.

Thomas refilled their water skins while Brynn unwrapped bread and cheese. They sat on rocks that lined the brook, eating in comfortable silence at first.

"Tell me again about the crown," Thomas finally said. "Your grandmother used to tell us those stories when we were children. I remember some of it, but you always remembered details better than I did. What did she say about how it was made?"

Brynn pulled out her grandmother's journal. She hadn't had time to read it properly yet—

yesterday had been too chaotic with preparations. Now seemed like the right moment.

"Let me see what grandmother actually wrote," she said, carefully opening the leather cover.

The pages were filled with her grandmother's precise, flowing script. Brynn turned carefully until she found a section titled "The Crimson Crown - A History."

"Here," she said, reading aloud. "The Crimson Crown was forged in the First Age, when magic flowed through the world as naturally as water flows downhill. The Celestial Smiths created it—beings of pure magic who could shape reality itself."

"What happened to them?" Thomas asked. "The Celestial Smiths?"

Brynn scanned further down the page. "Grandmother didn't know. She wrote that they vanished long ago, before human history began recording such things. All that remains are their works—the crown being the greatest, but not the only one." She looked up. "She mentions other artifacts, other powers hidden throughout the world."

"That's... both exciting and terrifying," Thomas said.

"The crown's purpose," Brynn continued reading, "was to bridge worlds—light and shadow, order and chaos, the physical and the magical. It was meant to maintain balance, to keep either side from overwhelming the other." She turned the page. "For centuries it passed from one guardian to the next, chosen not for power or nobility but for heart. For the capacity to balance mercy with justice, strength with compassion."

"Until when?" Thomas asked. "What stopped the succession?"

Brynn read ahead, then spoke quietly. "Until Lyra Stormblade. She was the last guardian."

"What happened to her?"

"She fought in the Shadow Wars," Brynn said, reading from the journal. "Against forces trying to claim the crown for darkness. In the end, to prevent its capture, she hid it with her dying breath and created the map that would reveal itself only to the next worthy guardian."

Thomas threw a pebble into the brook, watching ripples spread. "Which means your grandmother. But she never claimed it."

"No," Brynn agreed. "She never even tried, as far as I can tell. She lived her whole life in Thornhaven, married my grandfather, raised my mother." She paused, reading a particular passage. "But listen to this—she wrote: 'The crown must choose its time and its guardian. I was called, but my role was not to claim it. My role was to protect the map, to keep the stories alive, and to prepare the next guardian when she came.'"

"She knew it would be you," Thomas said quietly.

"Apparently." Brynn felt a lump in her throat. "She never told me directly. I found all of this after she died. But she was preparing me all along, wasn't she? With the stories, with the way she taught me to think and question."

"She was waiting," Thomas said. "Waiting for you to be ready."

They sat in silence for a moment, the weight of legacy settling around them.

"We should keep moving," Brynn finally said, closing the journal carefully. "According to the map, we still have several hours before we reach the first way marker."

The afternoon sun tracked their progress through gaps in the canopy. The forest began to change as they traveled—growing wilder, more untamed. These trees were even older, their bark scored with marks that might have been natural or might have been carved by hands unknown.

Around what Brynn judged to be late afternoon, they reached a clearing that stopped her in her tracks.

It was perfectly circular, perhaps fifty feet across, ringed by trees that seemed to lean inward as if listening. The grass inside was impossibly green, dotted with wildflowers that shouldn't bloom this early in autumn. And in the very center stood a single stone—not large, perhaps waist-high, but carved with symbols that matched those on her map.

"A way marker," Brynn breathed, approaching slowly.

Thomas circled the clearing's edge, examining everything with his practical eye. "This place was made, not naturally formed. Look at the way the trees are positioned—too perfect to be chance."

Brynn reached the stone and traced the carved symbols with her fingertips. They were warm to the touch, just like the map had been, and she felt that same sense of connection.

Words appeared in her mind, not heard but known: *First marker. Rest here. The path continues at dawn.*

"We're supposed to camp here," Brynn told Thomas. "I just... I know. The stone told me somehow."

"Convenient," Thomas said, though he didn't sound skeptical. "Or it could be a trap."

"It's not," Brynn said with certainty. "This place was made for travelers like us."

As evening approached, they made camp. Thomas gathered firewood while Brynn arranged their bedrolls and prepared a simple meal. By the time darkness fell properly, they had a cheerful fire and hot food.

The night sounds were strange—owls hooting in complex patterns, things rustling deliberately in the undergrowth, and occasionally howls that were neither wolf nor dog from somewhere far in the distance.

"We should keep watch," Thomas suggested. "I'll take first shift. You sleep."

Brynn wanted to argue, but exhaustion pulled at her. Walking all day with a heavy pack had taken more out of her than expected. "Wake me in four hours. I mean it this time."

"We'll see," Thomas said with a slight smile.

As Brynn settled into her bedroll, the fire's warmth on her face and stars visible through the clearing's opening, she felt that same profound sense of rightness she'd felt since finding the map. This was where she was meant to be.

Dreams came swiftly—visions of silver rivers and crystal mountains, voices speaking in languages she didn't know but somehow understood. And underlying it all, a presence watching, waiting, testing.

She woke sometime in the deep night to find Thomas had indeed let her sleep longer than four hours. The fire had burned low to embers, and Thomas sat with his back against a tree, sword across his knees, staring into the forest.

"You were supposed to wake me," Brynn said, sitting up.

"You needed the sleep more than I needed rest," Thomas replied. "Besides, I've been thinking."

"About?"

"About what we're doing. About the crown and this quest." He was quiet for a moment. "I touched that map because you asked me to. I heard the music and felt the pull. But Brynn, I'm not like you. I'm not destined for this. I'm just a blacksmith's son who follows his friend into trouble."

"You're more than that," Brynn said firmly.

"Maybe. But I'm here because of you. Because you needed someone and I couldn't let you go alone." Thomas finally turned to look at her. "What I'm trying to say is—whatever happens, whatever trials we face, I'm following your lead. You're the one the crown called."

"You heard the music too," Brynn reminded him. "That has to mean something."

"Or it just means I was standing next to you when you touched the map," Thomas said. "Either way, you're the guardian. I'm just here to help however I can."

"Then help by getting some sleep," Brynn said, moving to sit beside him. "I'll keep watch now."

Thomas nodded and settled into his bedroll. Within minutes his breathing deepened into sleep.

As Brynn kept watch, she thought about Thomas's words. What if he was right? What if the trials ahead were meant for one person, not two? The idea terrified her more than she wanted to admit.

No, she told herself. *We're in this together. That's how it has to be.*

The night passed slowly. Nothing threatened them, nothing emerged from the forest. But Brynn felt watched nonetheless, felt the forest's attention like a tangible presence.

When dawn finally began to lighten the eastern sky, she gently woke Thomas. They broke camp efficiently, extinguished the fire's remains, and shouldered their packs.

The way marker stone seemed to pulse as they prepared to leave, and again words appeared in Brynn's mind: *Northeast. Follow the song. The mountains wait.*

"This way," Brynn said, pointing. "Northeast. The stone says to follow the song."

"What song?" Thomas asked.

"I don't know yet," Brynn admitted. "But I think we'll know it when we hear it."

They left the clearing as the sun rose, painting the forest in shades of gold and green. The path ahead was unclear, unmapped in any literal sense. But the pull was there, gentle but insistent, drawing them forward.

The adventure had truly begun.

And whatever lay ahead—trials, dangers, wonders—they would face it together.

Chapter 3: Trials And Allies

The forest thinned gradually as they climbed, the dense canopy giving way to scattered pines and hardy shrubs that clung to increasingly rocky soil. By midmorning, Brynn and Thomas had left the ancient woods behind and found themselves on the lower slopes of the Misty Mountains, whose peaks rose before them like jagged teeth biting at the sky.

The change in terrain was dramatic. Gone were the soft forest paths and moss-covered stones. Here, the ground was hard and unforgiving, scattered with loose rocks that shifted treacherously underfoot. The air grew thinner and colder with each step upward, carrying the sharp scent of pine and stone.

"Look at that," Brynn said, stopping to catch her breath and pointing ahead.

Before them, a narrow path snaked up the mountainside, carved into the rock face itself. It looked ancient—worn smooth in places by centuries of use, yet also dangerous, with sections where the outer edge crumbled away into empty air.

"Someone made this path," Thomas observed, studying the deliberate way it switched back and forth across the steep slope. "A long time ago, but they made it for a purpose."

"For people seeking the altar," Brynn said, consulting the map. The parchment showed this exact location—the path winding up the mountain toward a point marked with a symbol that matched the way marker stone from last night. "We're close. The altar should be somewhere near the summit of this first peak."

Thomas adjusted his pack and tested the path with his boot. Loose stones skittered down the slope, disappearing into the mist that clung to the lower elevations. "Careful steps. One at a time. And stay away from the edge."

They began the ascent slowly, Thomas leading the way with Brynn close behind. The path was wider than it had appeared from below—just wide enough for two people to walk side by side if they were careful—but the drop-off on the outer edge was precipitous enough to make Brynn's stomach clench whenever she glanced that direction.

The climb was harder than anything they'd done in the forest. Each step required attention and effort. Loose stones threatened to turn ankles. The thinning air made breathing labored. Brynn's legs burned with exertion, and she could see sweat darkening Thomas's shirt despite the mountain chill.

They climbed for perhaps two hours before stopping to rest on a wider section of path where an outcropping of rock provided shelter from the wind that had begun to pick up.

"How much farther?" Thomas asked, breathing hard as he took a long drink from his water skin.

Brynn pulled out the map. "Hard to say. The map shows distance but not how long it takes to cover difficult terrain. But we're more than halfway, I think."

"Good," Thomas said. "Because I don't want to be on this path after dark."

Neither did Brynn. The thought of navigating these treacherous switchbacks in darkness made her shudder.

They had just shouldered their packs to continue when a sound stopped them both—a rustling in the scrub brush that clung to the mountainside above the path, too deliberate to be wind, too large to be a small animal.

Thomas's hand went immediately to his sword. "Did you hear that?" he asked quietly.

"Yes," Brynn whispered back, her own hand finding the knife at her belt.

The rustling came again, closer now. Rocks tumbled down from above, clattering across the path. And then a figure burst from the undergrowth —a man, wild-looking, with tangled hair and clothes that were more patches than original fabric. He brandished a gnarled walking staff like a weapon.

"Who goes there?" he shouted, his voice rough from disuse or the mountain air. "State your purpose!"

Brynn instinctively stepped in front of Thomas, hands raised to show they meant no harm. "We're travelers," she called back. "We mean no harm. We're just passing through."

The man narrowed his eyes, taking their measure. He was older than he'd first appeared— perhaps fifty, with a weathered face that spoke of years spent outdoors. His eyes were sharp and intelligent despite his ragged appearance.

"Travelers," he repeated skeptically. "On the old path. Heading toward the summit." He lowered the staff slightly but didn't relax his defensive posture. "Few come this way anymore. Most who do are seeking something they shouldn't seek."

"We're seeking the altar," Brynn said honestly. Something about this man made her think that lies would be pointless and possibly dangerous. "The ancient altar that's supposed to be near the peak."

The man's expression shifted—surprise mixed with something that might have been respect. "The altar," he said slowly. "Then you're either very brave or very foolish. Perhaps both." He studied them more carefully. "You don't look like treasure seekers. Too... earnest. And you," he pointed his staff at Brynn, "you have the look of someone called rather than someone seeking."

"Called?" Brynn asked.

"By something greater than yourself. I've seen that look before, many years ago." The man lowered his staff completely. "My name is Lucian. I've wandered these mountains longer than I care to remember. Long enough to know the altar and what it guards."

"What does it guard?" Thomas asked, speaking for the first time since the man's appearance.

Lucian's eyes shifted to Thomas, evaluating. "Truth. And those who can't bear truth don't survive the experience." He paused. "But you're already committed, aren't you? Already too far to turn back, even if you wanted to."

"We can't turn back," Brynn confirmed. "Will you help us? We could use someone who knows these mountains."

Lucian was quiet for a long moment, seeming to wrestle with some internal debate. Finally, he sighed. "Against my better judgment, yes. I'll guide you. But understand this—the journey ahead will change you. The altar tests those who approach it. Some pass. Some..." He left the sentence unfinished, the implication clear.

"We're ready," Brynn said, though her stomach tightened with nervousness.

"No one's ever ready," Lucian said. "But that's never stopped anyone who was truly called." He gestured up the path. "Come. We should reach the altar before nightfall if we don't waste time talking."

He set off at a pace that belied his ragged appearance, moving sure-footed over terrain that had Brynn and Thomas stepping carefully. They followed, grateful for his guidance as the path grew more treacherous.

As they climbed, Lucian spoke—not constantly, but in bursts of information that felt like gifts grudgingly given.

"The altar is old," he said at one point. "Older than the kingdoms, older than recorded history. It was built by those who understood that some knowledge requires preparation to receive. The unprepared are destroyed by what they learn."

"What kind of knowledge?" Brynn asked.

"That depends on the seeker," Lucian replied cryptically. "The altar shows each person what they need to see. Whether they can bear the seeing is another question entirely."

Later, when they stopped briefly for water, Lucian looked at the map Brynn had pulled out to check their progress.

"Interesting," he said, though he didn't ask to examine it more closely. "You carry something old.

Something that remembers what most have forgotten."

"You can sense it?" Brynn asked, surprised.

"I've spent too long in these mountains not to recognize power when I see it," Lucian said. "Power calls to power, magic to magic. Your map is more than parchment and ink."

"Do you know about the Crimson Crown?" Thomas asked.

Lucian's expression shifted—a flash of something that might have been pain or memory. "I know the stories. Everyone who wanders long enough in the forgotten places knows the stories. Whether the crown still exists, whether it can be found..." He shrugged. "That's a question I can't answer."

"But you believe it's possible," Brynn said, reading his tone.

"I believe many things are possible that most would call impossible," Lucian replied. "These mountains have taught me that the world is stranger and more magical than village-folk dare imagine."

The afternoon wore on. The path grew steeper, the air thinner. Brynn's lungs burned with each breath, and her legs felt like lead. Beside her, Thomas struggled equally, though he didn't complain.

Lucian, by contrast, seemed unaffected by the altitude or exertion, moving with the easy confidence of someone who'd made this climb countless times.

They were perhaps an hour from the summit when the first real danger appeared.

Brynn heard it before she saw it—a low growl that resonated in her chest, coming from somewhere above the path. She froze, hand going to her knife.

"Don't move," Lucian said quietly, his staff raised. "And whatever you do, don't look threatening."

From the rocks above, a creature emerged that made Brynn's breath catch. It was massive—easily the size of a large dog, but built more like a bear with elongated limbs and a coat of fur that seemed to absorb light rather than reflect it. Its eyes glowed faintly red, and its teeth, when it pulled back its lips in a snarl, were like daggers.

"Shadow beast," Lucian breathed. "They guard the approaches to places of power. This one's been here a long time."

The creature descended toward them with predatory grace, its growl deepening. Brynn could feel waves of wrongness emanating from it—this wasn't a natural animal but something twisted, corrupted.

"What do we do?" Thomas whispered, his sword half-drawn.

"It's testing us," Lucian said. "Gauging whether we're worthy to pass. If we fight, we prove we're no different from any other treasure seeker. If we run, we prove we're cowards. We need to show neither aggression nor fear."

"That's asking a lot," Brynn said, her heart hammering as the creature moved closer.

"The altar requires much," Lucian replied. "This is just the first test."

The shadow beast circled them slowly, its red eyes fixed on Brynn. She forced herself to meet its gaze, to project calm she didn't feel. Beside her, she could feel Thomas trembling with the effort of not drawing his weapon fully.

We mean no harm, Brynn thought, not knowing if the creature could understand but trying nonetheless. *We seek only what we're called to seek. We're not your enemy.*

The creature stopped circling. Its head tilted, studying her with an intelligence that was disturbingly human. Then, slowly, it backed away, retreating to the rocks above. With one final look at Brynn—assessment rather than threat—it disappeared into a crevice.

The tension broke. Thomas released a breath he'd been holding. "What just happened?"

"You passed the first test," Lucian said, looking at Brynn with new respect. "The beast sensed your intent. You carry no greed, no malice. Just purpose." He gestured up the path. "But don't relax yet. The closer we get to the altar, the stronger the guardians become."

They continued upward with renewed caution. The sun was descending toward the horizon, painting the sky in shades of orange and purple. Shadows lengthened across the mountainside.

Finally, as the last rays of direct sunlight touched the peaks above, they crested a rise and the altar came into view.

It stood in a natural amphitheater—a wide, flat area ringed by standing stones that seemed to hum with barely contained energy. The altar itself was at the center, a massive slab of black stone carved with symbols that glowed faintly in the fading light.

"There," Brynn breathed, feeling a pull toward the structure that was almost physical.

But between them and the altar stood more shadow beasts—at least a dozen, arranged in a semi-circle as if they'd been waiting. These were larger than the one they'd encountered on the path, more solid, more menacing.

And behind them, emerging from the shadows of the standing stones, came figures that made even Lucian take a step back.

They were humanoid but wrong—too tall, too thin, with movements that defied normal joint articulation. Their faces were featureless except for eyes that burned with cold blue fire. They wore armor that seemed to be made of shadow itself, constantly shifting and reforming.

"Shadow warriors," Lucian said, his voice tight with worry. "I've never seen them here before. Something's changed. Something's wrong."

"We have to reach the altar," Brynn said, her hand on the map inside her jacket. She could feel it pulsing, responding to the proximity of the ancient structure.

"Against those?" Thomas said, drawing his sword fully. "There are too many."

"Then we fight," Brynn said, drawing her knife. It felt inadequate against what they faced, but it was what she had.

Lucian looked at her, then at the shadow warriors, then back. Something shifted in his expression—decision made. "If you're truly called, truly worthy, then perhaps..." He raised his staff, and to Brynn's shock, it began to glow with its own light. "I haven't used this power in years. Swore I never would again. But some oaths can be broken for the right cause."

"You're a mage?" Thomas asked, shocked.

"Was," Lucian corrected. "A long time ago. Before I learned that power corrupts and magic demands terrible prices." He planted his staff. "But for this, for someone truly called to the crown, I'll pay that price one more time."

The shadow warriors advanced as one, silent and inexorable. The shadow beasts growled in unison, a sound that vibrated in Brynn's bones.

"Stay close," Lucian commanded. "And when I tell you to run for the altar, you run. Don't look back. Don't stop. Just run."

"We won't leave you—" Brynn started.

"You will," Lucian interrupted. "Because that's what I'm buying with this magic. Your chance to reach the altar. Don't waste it."

The shadow warriors reached striking distance. One lunged forward, its blade of solidified darkness aimed at Thomas. Lucian's staff blazed with light, and a barrier of pure radiance sprang up between them and their attackers.

"Now!" Lucian shouted. "Run!"

Brynn hesitated for a heartbeat, seeing the strain on Lucian's face as he held the barrier against the onslaught. Then Thomas grabbed her arm.

"Come on!" he yelled. "Don't make his sacrifice meaningless!"

They ran.

Behind them, Brynn heard the sounds of battle—the crack of magic against magic, Lucian's shouts of effort and pain, the inhuman screeches of the shadow creatures. Every instinct screamed at her to turn back, to help, but Thomas pulled her forward.

They sprinted across the amphitheater, dodging between standing stones. A shadow beast broke through Lucian's barrier and lunged at them. Thomas met it with his sword, the blade catching it mid-leap and sending it tumbling aside with a cry of pain.

The altar was close now. Twenty feet. Fifteen. Ten.

Another shadow warrior materialized directly in their path. Brynn didn't think, didn't plan—she just acted. Drawing on something deep inside her, something that had awakened when she touched the map, she thrust her hand forward and shouted wordlessly.

Light burst from her palm—not as strong as Lucian's magic, but enough. The shadow warrior recoiled, giving them the seconds they needed.

Five feet. Three.

They reached the altar and collapsed against it, gasping. The moment Brynn's hand touched the black stone, everything changed.

A dome of pure white light erupted from the altar, expanding outward to encompass the entire amphitheater. The shadow creatures shrieked and dissolved where the light touched them, unable to withstand its purity.

In seconds, the threat was gone. Only Lucian remained, slumped against his staff, his face drawn with exhaustion but alive.

The light from the altar faded to a gentle glow, and Brynn heard words in her mind, clearer than before: *The first trial is complete. You have proven your worth. Rest now. The true test comes at dawn.*

Brynn looked at Thomas, who stared back at her with wide eyes. They'd made it. Against impossible odds, they'd reached the altar.

But as she looked at Lucian, struggling to stand, she knew the victory had come at a cost.

And tomorrow's test, whatever it might be, would be even harder.

Chapter 4: The Altar's Test

The night passed in uneasy vigilance.

Lucian had collapsed shortly after the barrier fell, his breathing shallow and labored. Thomas helped Brynn move him closer to the altar, where the residual warmth from the stone seemed to ease his distress somewhat. They made camp in the protection of the standing stones, building a small fire with dried brush Thomas found wedged between rocks.

"Will he be alright?" Brynn asked, kneeling beside Lucian's still form. His face was pale, drawn, and she could see tremors running through his limbs.

"Magic takes its toll," Lucian whispered, his eyes still closed. "Especially when you've forsworn it for years. The price... is always higher than you remember."

"Rest," Thomas said firmly. "We'll keep watch."

Brynn pulled her blanket over Lucian, tucking it around his shoulders. He'd saved their lives.

Whatever test awaited them at dawn, they owed him everything.

Thomas took first watch while Brynn tried to sleep, but rest wouldn't come easily. Every time she closed her eyes, she saw those shadow warriors advancing, felt the surge of power that had erupted from her palm when she'd thrust her hand forward. That light hadn't come from nowhere—it had come from within her, from some reservoir she hadn't known existed.

What am I becoming? she wondered, staring up at the stars visible between the standing stones. *Is this what the crown does to its guardians? Or is this something that was always inside me, just waiting to be awakened?*

Around midnight, she gave up on sleep and relieved Thomas, sending him to rest. The mountain night was cold but beautiful—the sky so clear that the stars seemed close enough to touch, the Milky Way a river of light overhead.

Brynn sat with her back against the altar stone, feeling its warmth seep into her shoulders. The symbols carved into its surface glowed faintly, pulsing in rhythm with something she couldn't quite identify. Her heartbeat? The earth's own pulse? Both seemed possible here, in this place where the boundary between mundane and magical felt thin as paper.

She pulled out her grandmother's journal and, by the light of the dying fire and the altar's glow, began to read.

The pages were filled with more than just information about the crown. Her grandmother had written personal reflections, questions, doubts. One passage in particular caught Brynn's attention:

"The calling is both gift and burden. To be chosen means accepting that your life is no longer entirely your own. The crown's purpose becomes your purpose. Its mission becomes your mission. I felt this calling at twenty-three, standing where you now stand (for I know you will read this at the altar, granddaughter—the map ensures it). I felt the power waiting to be claimed, felt the crown reaching out across distance and time."

Brynn's breath caught. Her grandmother had been here. Had stood exactly where Brynn now sat.

She read on:

"But I also felt something else—a vision of a different path. I saw a child, not yet born, who would carry the calling forward with greater strength than I possessed. I saw you, Brynn, though I didn't know your name then. I knew only that my role was to wait, to preserve, to prepare the way. So I walked away from the altar without claiming what it offered. The hardest decision of my life, but the right one."

Tears blurred Brynn's vision. Her grandmother had sacrificed her own destiny for Brynn's sake. Had lived an ordinary life in Thornhaven when she could have wielded power beyond imagining.

"Do not mourn my choice," the next line read, as if anticipating Brynn's reaction. *"I lived a good life. I loved your grandfather. I raised your mother. I watched you grow into the woman I knew you would become. These are not small things. And now, at the end, I can pass this calling to you with a peaceful heart, knowing you are ready for what I was not."*

"What are you reading?" a quiet voice asked.

Brynn looked up to find Lucian awake, watching her with eyes that reflected the altar's glow.

"My grandmother's journal," Brynn said, closing it carefully. "She was here. At this altar. Twenty-some years ago."

"Meredith," Lucian said, and Brynn's head snapped up in shock.

"You knew her?" Brynn asked.

"I knew of her," Lucian said, sitting up slowly, wincing with the effort. "A young woman came to the altar the year I arrived in these mountains. She touched the stone, underwent the vision, and then... walked away. I never understood why. Most who reach this place are consumed by the need to continue, to claim what they seek. But she simply left."

"She saw me," Brynn said softly. "In the vision. She saw that I was meant to be here instead."

Lucian studied her face in the dim light. "Then she was wiser than most. The crown doesn't just choose guardians—it chooses the right guardian for the right time. Your grandmother understood that."

"What happens at dawn?" Brynn asked. "The altar said the true test comes then. What does that mean?"

"The altar shows you truth," Lucian said. "About yourself, about your purpose, about what you're capable of. Some people can't bear what they see. They break under the weight of self-knowledge." He paused. "But I don't think you will. You have your grandmother's strength. I saw that tonight, when you faced the shadow warriors."

"I didn't know I could do that," Brynn admitted. "That light that came from my hand—I've never done anything like that before."

"The calling awakens what's dormant," Lucian said. "The closer you get to the crown, the more your true nature emerges. By the time you stand before it, you'll be fully what you were always meant to be."

"And if I'm not strong enough? If the crown rejects me?"

"Then it rejects you," Lucian said bluntly. "But I've been watching you since we met on the path. I've seen how you move, how you think, how you lead without realizing you're leading. You're not like the others who've come seeking the crown—the power-hungry, the ambitious, the desperate. You're here because you were called. That makes all the difference."

Thomas stirred from sleep, sitting up and rubbing his eyes. "What time is it?" he asked.

"A few hours before dawn," Brynn said.

"You should go back to sleep," Thomas said. "You need more rest."

"So do you," Brynn replied. She looked at Lucian. "How are you feeling?"

"Like I've been trampled by horses and left for dead," Lucian said with a weak smile. "But I'll survive. I always do, somehow."

"Thank you," Thomas said seriously. "For what you did. We wouldn't have made it without you."

Lucian waved the thanks away. "I did what needed doing. Besides, it's been years since I felt useful. Worth the pain, almost."

They sat together in companionable silence, watching the stars wheel slowly overhead and waiting for dawn. Brynn felt a strange sense of peace despite the uncertainty ahead. Whatever the altar showed her, whatever test it demanded, she would face it. Not because she was particularly brave or strong, but because refusing felt impossible. The calling Lucian and her grandmother spoke of wasn't something you could walk away from, even if you wanted to.

And she didn't want to.

The sky began to lighten gradually, the black of night fading to deep blue, then purple, then pink. Birds Brynn hadn't known lived at this altitude began to sing, their calls echoing between the standing stones.

As the first direct rays of sunlight touched the altar, it began to glow more brightly. The symbols carved into its surface blazed with golden light, and a sound like a bell being struck resonated through the amphitheater.

It is time, a voice said—not in Brynn's mind but all around them, seeming to come from the stones themselves. *Step forward, seeker. Face what must be faced. See what must be seen.*

Brynn stood, her legs trembling slightly. Thomas stood too, moving to follow her.

"No," Lucian said, catching Thomas's arm. "This part she must do alone. The altar's vision is personal. Private. We can only wait."

Thomas looked torn, but he nodded and stepped back. "Be careful," he said to Brynn.

"Always am," Brynn replied with a confidence she didn't entirely feel.

She approached the altar slowly, each step feeling weighted with significance. When she was close enough to touch the black stone, she hesitated, her hand hovering inches from its surface.

Do not fear what you will see, the voice said. *Truth is not your enemy, even when it's painful. Place your hand upon the stone and open yourself to what is.*

Brynn took a deep breath and pressed her palm flat against the altar.

The world exploded into light.

She was no longer standing on the mountain. She was everywhere and nowhere, suspended in a space that wasn't space, surrounded by images that flashed past faster than thought.

She saw herself as a child, sitting at her grandmother's feet while the old woman told stories by firelight. Saw herself learning to read, to think, to question. Saw her grandmother shaping her deliberately, preparing her for a destiny she couldn't yet understand.

She saw her parents—her mother's disappointment that Brynn spent more time with her grandmother than learning practical skills, her father's quiet pride in her curiosity and courage. Saw the moment they'd died in the accident that had left her in her grandmother's care permanently, saw the grief that had shaped her as much as love had.

She saw Thomas—her best friend since childhood, loyal and steady. But she also saw something she'd never fully acknowledged: the way he looked at her when he thought she wasn't watching, the depth of feeling he kept carefully hidden because he valued her friendship too much to risk it.

She saw Thornhaven from above, saw its simple beauty and also its limitations. Saw the life she could have lived if she'd never found the map— comfortable, safe, small. Married to a local boy (Thomas, probably), running a shop or tending children, growing old in the same place she'd grown up.

It wasn't a bad life. But it wasn't her life. Not the one she was meant for.

The visions shifted. She saw the crown itself—not a physical object but an idea made manifest, a promise of balance and power and terrible responsibility. Saw the guardians who'd come before, each one facing impossible choices, each one sacrificing parts of themselves to maintain the balance the crown represented.

She saw Lyra Stormblade—fierce and brilliant and ultimately alone, fighting a battle she knew she couldn't win, hiding the crown with her dying breath not out of defeat but out of hope that someone better would find it.

She saw her grandmother again, young and strong, standing where Brynn now stood, feeling the crown's call. Saw her vision of Brynn, the decision to walk away, the years of waiting and wondering if she'd made the right choice.

She did, Brynn thought with certainty. *She made exactly the right choice.*

The visions shifted again, showing her possible futures—not predictions but potentials. Paths she might walk, choices she might make.

In one, she claimed the crown and became a guardian of terrible power, wielding magic that could reshape reality. But the cost was clear—isolation, loneliness, the weight of decisions no mortal should have to make.

In another, she reached the crown but couldn't claim it, her heart too divided, her purpose too uncertain. She returned to Thornhaven, lived the comfortable life, but always wondered what she'd given up.

In a third, she claimed the crown but let its power corrupt her, became the very thing the guardians were supposed to prevent—a tyrant wielding absolute authority, convinced her vision of balance was the only correct one.

And in a fourth... in a fourth, she claimed the crown and bore its burden wisely, balancing power with humility, strength with compassion. She didn't fight alone—Thomas was there, and others, and together they protected the balance without being consumed by it.

Choose, the voice said. *Not the path—that comes later, with each decision you make. But choose who you are. Choose what you value. Choose what matters most.*

Brynn saw her reflection in a mirror that wasn't a mirror—saw herself not as she was but as she could be. All the potential versions of herself layered over one another, waiting to be chosen or rejected.

She thought about her grandmother's sacrifice, about Thomas's loyalty, about Lucian's pain-bought wisdom. She thought about the shadow beasts and shadow warriors, about the power she'd felt surge through her when she'd needed it most.

And she thought about the crown—not as an object to possess but as a responsibility to bear.

I am Brynn Thornwick, she thought clearly, projecting the words into the vision space around her. Granddaughter of Meredith, friend of Thomas, seeker of the Crimson Crown. I'm not perfect. I'm not particularly powerful. But I'm called, and I accept that calling. Not for glory or power, but because it's what I'm meant to do. I'll make mistakes. I'll doubt. But I won't give up. And I won't face this alone.

The vision space blazed with light so bright it should have been painful but wasn't. Brynn felt something settle into place deep in her chest—not a physical thing but a certainty, a commitment made and accepted.

You have chosen well, the voice said. *You have seen yourself truly and not turned away. The first trial is now complete. The second trial lies ahead, beyond the Fang Mountains and the silver river. Go with my blessing, seeker. May your heart remain true.*

The light faded. Brynn found herself standing at the altar, her hand still pressed against its surface. The sun was higher now—at least an hour had passed, though it had felt like moments.

She turned to find Thomas and Lucian watching anxiously.

"I'm alright," she said, though her voice shook slightly. "I'm... I'm alright."

Thomas crossed to her in three quick strides and pulled her into a hug. "You were glowing," he said into her hair. "The whole time, you were glowing like the sun."

"I saw things," Brynn said softly. "True things. Hard things. But necessary things."

"And?" Lucian asked.

"And I'm ready," Brynn said, pulling back from Thomas and standing straight. "For whatever comes next. I'm ready."

The altar's glow faded to nothing, its purpose fulfilled. The standing stones around them seemed less imposing now, more welcoming.

"Then we should move on," Lucian said. "The altar has shown you your path. The next waypoint is days away, and the journey will only get harder."

"You're coming with us?" Thomas asked.

Lucian smiled—a real smile this time, not the bitter one he'd worn when they first met. "Someone needs to keep you two alive. And besides, I've spent years hiding in these mountains, avoiding my past. Maybe it's time I stopped running and did something that matters again."

Brynn looked at her two companions—Thomas, who'd followed her into danger without question, and Lucian, who'd sacrificed his safety to protect them. She felt a surge of gratitude and determination.

"Then let's go," she said. "The crown is waiting. And we have a long way to travel."

They gathered their supplies, extinguished their fire, and left the altar behind. As they descended the mountain on the far side—a gentler slope than the one they'd climbed—Brynn looked back once.

The amphitheater was empty now, peaceful in the morning light. But she knew it would always be there, testing those who sought the crown, showing them truths they might not want to see but needed to understand.

She turned forward again, toward the path ahead, toward the unknown.

The first trial was complete.

But the journey had only just begun.

Chapter 5: The Descent And The River

The descent from the altar proved easier than the climb had been, though no less significant. The path on this side of the mountain was wider, less treacherous, winding through stands of pine and over smooth granite that had been worn by centuries of weather and footsteps.

As they walked, Brynn felt different—lighter somehow, despite the weight of what she'd seen in the vision. The altar had shown her truths about herself, some comfortable and some not, but knowing them felt better than the uncertainty she'd carried before.

"You're quiet," Thomas observed after they'd been walking for perhaps an hour. He fell into step beside her while Lucian ranged ahead, his staff tapping a steady rhythm on the stone path.

"Thinking," Brynn said. "About what I saw. About what it means."

"Do you want to talk about it?" Thomas asked.

Brynn considered. The vision had been personal, intimate—the altar had shown her things she'd barely admitted to herself. But Thomas deserved to know at least some of it. He'd followed her into this quest without hesitation. He'd earned her trust.

"I saw possible futures," she said carefully. "Different paths I might walk. Some good. Some... less so."

"And which one did you choose?" Thomas asked.

"That's the thing," Brynn said. "I didn't choose a specific future. The altar said I was choosing who I am, not what happens. It's like..." She struggled to find the words. "It's like the altar wanted me to know myself well enough that whatever comes, I'll make the right choices. Does that make sense?"

"I think so," Thomas said. "Know yourself and you'll know what to do when the moment comes."

"Exactly." Brynn was quiet for a moment, then added, "I saw you. In the vision. In most of the futures, you were there with me."

Thomas's expression shifted—something hopeful and vulnerable crossing his face before he schooled it back to his usual steady calm. "Most?" he asked lightly.

"The bad ones, you weren't there," Brynn admitted. "The futures where I failed or became corrupted or gave up—in those, I was alone. It made me realize..." She paused, choosing her words carefully. "I need you, Thomas. Not just for this quest, but for what comes after. You keep me grounded. You keep me human."

"Then I'm not going anywhere," Thomas said simply. "No matter what."

They walked in comfortable silence after that, the unspoken things between them acknowledged if not fully addressed. Brynn knew there were deeper conversations they would need to have eventually—about feelings and futures and what came after the crown. But for now, this was enough.

By midday they'd descended below the tree line again, entering a forest of tall pines whose needles carpeted the ground in a soft, rust-colored blanket. The air here smelled of resin and earth, and the temperature was noticeably warmer than it had been at altitude.

Lucian called a halt in a small clearing where a spring bubbled up from between rocks, forming a clear pool before trickling away downhill.

"We should rest and eat," he said, settling onto a convenient boulder with a grunt. "And we should talk about what comes next."

Brynn and Thomas unpacked their food—bread that was getting slightly stale, cheese that had softened in the warm air, and dried fruit that Lucian contributed from his own supplies. They ate while Lucian pulled out a rough map he'd drawn on a piece of leather.

"We're here," he said, pointing to a spot marked with an X. "The altar. Our destination is here—" he moved his finger northeast across the leather "—beyond the Fang Mountains, past the silver river, in a place the old maps call the Crystal Valley."

"That's where the crown is?" Thomas asked.

"According to legend," Lucian said. "But getting there won't be simple. We have perhaps five days of relatively easy travel through these foothills. Then we reach the Fang Mountains—a more treacherous range than what we just crossed. Sharp peaks, narrow passes, unpredictable weather."

"And the silver river?" Brynn asked, consulting her own map. The parchment showed the river as a gleaming line that seemed to actually shimmer on the page.

"A barrier as much as a landmark," Lucian said. "The river flows from the heart of the mountains, and its waters have... properties. Some say drinking from it grants visions. Others say it drives you mad. I've never been that far myself, but I've heard stories."

"Encouraging," Thomas muttered.

"The path of the crown was never meant to be easy," Lucian said. "Each challenge is a test. Each obstacle a way of proving you're worthy." He looked at Brynn. "But you've passed the first trial. That's more than most manage."

"What about the second trial?" Brynn asked. "The altar said it lies ahead. Do you know what it is?"

Lucian shook his head. "The trials are different for each seeker. What tests one person might not test another. But I can tell you this—the first trial was about knowing yourself. The second, if the old stories are true, is about knowing others. About trust and alliance and understanding that no guardian stands alone."

Brynn thought about the vision she'd seen—the futures where she succeeded, Thomas and others had been beside her. The futures where she failed, she'd been isolated, solitary. "Then we're already on the right path," she said. "Because I'm not doing this alone."

They finished their meal and continued downward. The forest grew denser as they descended, the pines giving way to mixed hardwoods—oak and ash and maple that were just beginning to show autumn colors. The path became less defined here, forcing them to navigate by Lucian's knowledge and Brynn's map.

As afternoon faded toward evening, they heard water—not the trickle of a spring but the rush of a substantial stream. Following the sound, they emerged from the trees onto the bank of a river perhaps thirty feet wide, flowing fast and clear over a bed of smooth stones.

"We'll camp here tonight," Lucian announced, surveying the area with an experienced eye. "Good water, defensible position, and we can follow the river downstream tomorrow. It should lead us toward the Fang Mountains."

They made camp with the efficiency of practice, Thomas gathering firewood while Brynn cleared a space for their bedrolls and Lucian used his staff to draw what looked like protective symbols in the dirt around their campsite.

"Is that magic?" Thomas asked, watching the symbols glow faintly before fading to nothing.

"Simple wards," Lucian said. "They won't stop anything truly determined, but they'll alert us if something crosses the boundary. And they might discourage opportunistic predators."

As twilight deepened, they sat around their fire, the river's rushing providing a constant backdrop. Brynn found herself studying her companions in the flickering light. Thomas, reliable and strong, his face showing the strain of the journey but his determination unshaken. Lucian, mysterious and scarred by whatever past he'd fled, but clearly knowledgeable and committed to their cause.

"Tell me something," Brynn said, breaking the comfortable silence. "Both of you. Why are you really here? Thomas, you could have stayed in Thornhaven, taken over your father's forge, lived a good life. And Lucian, you could have stayed hidden in your mountains. So why?"

Thomas spoke first. "I'm here because you're here," he said simply. "I've been following you since we were eight years old, Brynn. Into scrapes, into trouble, into adventures. This is just... a bigger adventure than usual." He smiled slightly. "Besides, what kind of friend would I be if I let you face this alone?"

"And you?" Brynn asked Lucian.

The older man was quiet for a long moment, staring into the fire. When he spoke, his voice was heavy with old regret. "I told you I was a mage once. What I didn't tell you was why I stopped. Why I fled to the mountains and swore never to use magic again."

Neither Brynn nor Thomas spoke, waiting for him to continue at his own pace.

"I had a wife," Lucian said finally. "And a daughter. We lived in a city far from here, and I was respected, powerful. People came to me for help, and I gave it freely. I thought I was doing good." He paused. "Then one day, a man came asking me to curse his enemy. I refused, of course. But he persisted, offered gold, made threats. Finally, he attacked me in my own home."

Lucian's hands tightened on his staff. "I defended myself. Used magic without thinking, without restraint. The spell I cast..." He closed his eyes. "It didn't just kill him. It consumed him and everything around him. My home. My workshop. And my family, who were in the wrong place at the wrong moment."

"Oh, Lucian," Brynn whispered.

"I've spent twenty years in those mountains," Lucian continued, "trying to atone for what I did. Trying to become powerless so I could never hurt anyone again. But when I saw you two on that path, saw the shadow beasts and warriors, I realized something—refusing to use power when it's needed is its own kind of sin. My family wouldn't have wanted me to waste my life in isolation. They would have wanted me to use what I have to protect others."

"So that's why you helped us," Thomas said quietly.

"That's why I'm still helping you," Lucian said. "This quest, this crown—it matters. It's something worth using power for. Worth taking risks for. And maybe, if I help you succeed, I can balance the scales a little. Make up for what I destroyed."

Brynn reached across the fire and took Lucian's hand. "You already have," she said. "You saved our lives. You've guided us. You've shared your knowledge. That matters, Lucian. That counts."

Lucian squeezed her hand briefly before pulling away, clearly uncomfortable with the emotion. "Well," he said gruffly. "Enough maudlin talk. We should sleep. Tomorrow we have a long walk ahead."

They arranged their watch schedule—Lucian first, then Thomas, then Brynn. As she settled into her bedroll, Brynn found herself thinking about what Lucian had said. About power and responsibility, about atonement and purpose.

The crown she sought wasn't just an artifact. It was a burden, a calling, a terrible responsibility. But it was also a chance to do good, to protect balance, to make a difference.

I'm ready, she thought as sleep claimed her. *Whatever comes next, I'm ready.*

Her dreams were quieter than they'd been at the altar—just images of flowing water and distant mountains, peaceful and promising.

She woke to Thomas gently shaking her shoulder. "Your watch," he whispered.

Brynn took her position by the fire, feeding it carefully to keep it alive. The night was clear and cool, stars brilliant overhead. The river rushed past in its eternal journey, and somewhere in the distance, an owl called.

She pulled out her grandmother's journal, reading by firelight. There was a section she hadn't gotten to yet, near the back of the book.

"If you've reached this page, you've passed the first trial," her grandmother had written. *"You've seen yourself truly and not turned away. I'm proud of you, though I won't be there to tell you so in person."*

Brynn felt tears prick her eyes.

"The journey ahead will be harder. The second trial will test your bonds with others, your ability to trust and be trusted. Remember this: the crown's power is not meant to be wielded alone. Every guardian who tried to carry the burden solo either

failed or was corrupted. You will need allies, friends, people who keep you honest and human."

Brynn looked at Thomas and Lucian, sleeping peacefully nearby.

"It looks like you've already found them," her grandmother's next line read, as if anticipating Brynn's thoughts. *"Trust them. Lean on them. Let them lean on you. The strongest guardian is not the one who stands alone, but the one who knows when to accept help."*

Brynn closed the journal carefully and tucked it away. Her grandmother's wisdom continued to guide her even in death, preparing her for what lay ahead.

Dawn came gradually, painting the sky in shades of rose and gold. They broke camp, extinguished their fire, and began following the river downstream.

The path was easier here, the riverbank providing a natural route through the forest. They made good time, covering what Lucian estimated was ten miles by midday.

Around noon, they encountered their first sign that they weren't alone in these woods. Footprints in the soft earth near the riverbank—human footprints, fairly fresh, heading in the same direction they were traveling.

"Someone else is out here," Thomas observed, kneeling to examine the tracks more closely. "Moving fast. Alone, I think."

"Running from something or running toward something," Lucian said. "Either way, we should be cautious."

They continued more carefully, hands near weapons, eyes scanning the forest around them. The river grew wider and faster as tributaries joined it, the sound of rushing water becoming a constant roar.

Late in the afternoon, they found the source of the footprints.

A young woman sat on a boulder beside the river, her head in her hands. She wore travel-stained clothing and carried a pack that looked as battered as she did. At the sound of their approach, her head snapped up, hand going to a knife at her belt.

"Peace," Brynn called, raising her hands to show they meant no harm. "We're just travelers. Are you alright?"

The woman studied them warily. She was perhaps twenty, with dark hair pulled back in a practical braid and eyes that held a mixture of exhaustion and determination. "That depends on your definition of alright," she said. "I'm alive. I'm not injured. But I'm definitely not where I intended to be."

"Lost?" Thomas asked.

"More like... diverted," the woman said. She seemed to make a decision and lowered her knife. "My name is Kira. I was traveling with a merchant caravan, heading for the eastern settlements. Three days ago, we were attacked by bandits. I escaped into the forest and I've been trying to find my way back to civilization ever since."

"You're going the wrong way," Lucian said bluntly. "This river flows toward the mountains, not toward settled lands."

Kira's shoulders sagged. "Of course it does. My luck has been terrible lately." She looked at them more carefully. "Where are you three headed?"

"Northeast," Brynn said, not elaborating. "Toward the Fang Mountains."

"You're insane," Kira said flatly. "Those mountains are dangerous. Unpredictable weather, treacherous terrain, and stories of creatures that shouldn't exist."

"We know," Thomas said. "We're going anyway."

Kira laughed—a sound without humor. "Well, I suppose following insane people toward dangerous mountains is better than wandering lost in the forest. Mind if I tag along until we reach somewhere I can get proper directions?"

Brynn exchanged glances with Thomas and Lucian. This was unexpected. But something about Kira felt right—her directness, her practical nature, even her self-deprecating humor about her situation.

The second trial will test your bonds with others, her grandmother's journal had said. *Your ability to trust and be trusted.*

"You can travel with us," Brynn said. "But understand, we're not turning back. We're going all the way to the mountains and beyond. If you come with us, you come all the way."

Kira studied Brynn's face, seeming to recognize the seriousness behind the words. "What are you looking for in those mountains?" she asked.

"Something important," Brynn said. "Something worth risking everything for."

Kira was quiet for a moment, then nodded slowly. "Alright. I'll come with you. I don't have anywhere better to be, and honestly, you seem more competent than I've been managing on my own." She stood, shouldering her pack. "But if we're traveling together, I should warn you—I'm no fighter. I can use this knife in a pinch, but I'm better at talking my way out of trouble than fighting my way out."

"We could use someone who can talk," Thomas said with a slight smile. "We've been doing a lot of fighting lately."

"Then it's settled," Lucian said. "Four instead of three. Let's keep moving. We want to make good distance before nightfall."

As they set off along the river, Brynn fell into step beside their new companion. "Tell me about yourself," she said. "What were you doing with a merchant caravan?"

"Working," Kira said. "I'm a translator. I speak six languages, which makes me useful for caravans trading across different regions. Or it did, until the bandits attacked." She shook her head. "I've spent my whole life traveling, never staying anywhere long. It seemed like a good life until recently."

"What changed?" Brynn asked.

"I started wondering if there was more," Kira said. "More than just translating contracts and helping merchants haggle. Something meaningful. Something that mattered." She glanced at Brynn. "Which is probably why I agreed to follow you so easily. Whatever you're looking for, it's clearly meaningful to you. That's attractive to someone who's been feeling adrift."

"Just so you know," Brynn said, "what we're seeking is dangerous. People have died pursuing it. And even if we succeed, the burden that comes with it..." She trailed off, unsure how to explain the crown's weight to someone who didn't know about it.

"Everything worth having comes with a price," Kira said simply. "I learned that early. The question is whether the price is worth paying. And whether you're willing to pay it."

Brynn found herself liking this strange young woman they'd found by the river. There was something refreshing about her directness, her willingness to embrace uncertainty.

The second trial, she thought. *About trust and alliance. Maybe Kira is part of that test. Maybe learning to trust someone new, someone we just met, is exactly what we need to prove.*

As the sun set behind the mountains to the west, painting the sky in spectacular shades of orange and purple, they made camp beside the river once more. But this time, there were four of them around the fire instead of three.

The journey was getting more complicated.

But somehow, Brynn thought it was also getting richer.

Chapter 6: Bonds And Betrayals

The addition of Kira to their group changed the dynamic in ways both subtle and obvious.

She was talkative where Lucian was reserved, curious where Thomas was cautious, and possessed a quick wit that kept them entertained during the long hours of walking. By the second day of traveling together, it felt like she'd been with them from the beginning.

"So let me understand this correctly," Kira said as they followed the river through a narrow gorge, the water rushing white and furious below them. "You found a magical map in your dead grandmother's attic, it showed you visions when you touched it, and now you're following it to find an ancient crown that may or may not exist?"

"That's... essentially accurate," Brynn admitted.

"And you," Kira turned to Thomas, "you're a blacksmith who decided to abandon your livelihood and follow your best friend on this impossible quest because...?"

"Because she needed me," Thomas said simply.

"And you," Kira addressed Lucian, "you're a former mage who swore off magic twenty years ago but broke that vow to save these two from shadow monsters?"

"Also accurate," Lucian said dryly.

Kira shook her head in apparent amazement. "I've traveled with merchants, scholars, soldiers, and once a very strange group of performing acrobats. But you three are by far the most interesting traveling companions I've ever had."

"Is that a compliment?" Thomas asked.

"I haven't decided yet," Kira replied with a grin. "Ask me again when we either find this crown or die trying."

Despite her levity, Kira proved useful in practical ways. She had an uncanny ability to find the best campsites, could identify edible plants that supplemented their dwindling food supplies, and her six languages included an ancient tongue that helped decipher some of the symbols on Brynn's map.

Three days after Kira joined them, they reached a point where the river split around a large island, creating two channels. Lucian studied both options with a frown.

"The map shows we need to cross the river soon," Brynn said, consulting the glowing parchment. "But I can't tell which channel would be better."

"The left channel is narrower," Thomas observed. "Might be easier to ford."

"But the right channel flows slower," Kira pointed out. "Less chance of being swept away."

"We could split up," Lucian suggested. "Two take each channel, meet on the other side of the island, share what we find."

Brynn felt a prickle of unease at the suggestion. Something about separating felt wrong, though she couldn't articulate why.

"I don't think we should split up," she said carefully.

"It would save time," Lucian pressed. "We could scout both routes, determine the best crossing point."

"Brynn's right," Thomas said. "We stay together. That's been working for us so far."

Lucian looked like he wanted to argue but ultimately nodded. "The right channel then. Slower water means safer crossing."

They worked their way around to the right channel and found a spot where the river widened and shallowed, the current still strong but manageable. Thomas went first, his greater weight and strength making him the natural choice to test the crossing.

The water came up to his thighs in the deepest part, and he had to brace himself against the current, but he made it across without incident. Lucian went next, using his staff for balance, then Kira, who was lighter but nimbler than she appeared.

Brynn went last. Halfway across, her foot slipped on a moss-covered stone and she stumbled. The current grabbed her, pulling her downstream. She heard Thomas shout and saw him running along the far bank, but the water had her now, tumbling her head over heels.

She managed to keep her head up enough to breathe, fighting against the current while trying to angle toward the shore. The river swept her around a bend and suddenly she was in calmer water, able to get her feet under her and stumble toward the bank.

Strong hands grabbed her arms, pulling her onto dry land. She lay gasping on the rocky shore, coughing up river water.

"Are you hurt?" It was Kira's voice, urgent with concern.

"I'm fine," Brynn managed. "Just... give me a minute."

She heard splashing and looked up to see Thomas wading into the shallows, having run along the bank to reach her. Lucian appeared moments later, breathing hard from the sprint.

"You scared us," Thomas said, kneeling beside her. "When you went under—"

"I'm okay," Brynn assured him. She sat up slowly, checking herself for injuries. Everything hurt, but nothing seemed broken or seriously damaged. Her pack was still on her back, waterlogged but intact.

"The map," she said suddenly, panic flooding through her. "The journal—"

She pulled off her pack and frantically opened it. The leather journal was soaked but seemed intact. And the map... she pulled it out carefully, expecting to find the magical parchment ruined by water.

Instead, it was completely dry. Not a drop of moisture on it, as if it had been wrapped in something waterproof, though Brynn knew it hadn't been.

"Magic," Lucian said, seeing her expression. "The map protects itself. It wants to be found, wants to guide you. A little river water won't damage it."

Brynn carefully repacked the map and journal, her hands shaking slightly from the adrenaline. "We should keep moving," she said. "I'm fine, really. Just shaken."

They continued along the river, but the near-drowning had sobered everyone. The easy camaraderie of the morning felt strained, replaced by a more cautious wariness.

That night, they made camp in a cave Kira found—a shallow overhang that provided shelter from a light rain that had begun to fall. They built their fire near the cave's entrance, the smoke curling up and out while the flames provided warmth and light.

"Tell me about this crown," Kira said as they ate a meager dinner of dried meat and the edible tubers she'd found earlier. "I mean, I know you're looking for it, but what is it? What does it do?"

Brynn glanced at Thomas and Lucian, silently asking if they should share this. Thomas shrugged—the decision was hers. Lucian seemed neutral.

"The Crimson Crown," Brynn began, "was forged in the First Age by beings called Celestial Smiths. It's meant to maintain balance—between light and shadow, order and chaos, the physical and magical worlds."

"And it chooses guardians," Kira said, understanding dawning. "That's why you're seeking it. You think it's chosen you."

"I know it has," Brynn said. "I've felt it calling since I touched the map. And the altar—the first trial—confirmed it."

"Trials?" Kira asked. "There are tests?"

"The altar was the first," Brynn explained. "It showed me truths about myself. The second trial is supposed to be ahead somewhere, though I don't know exactly where or what it will test."

Kira was quiet for a long moment, staring into the fire. "And when you find this crown, what happens? You just... take it? Become its guardian?"

"If I'm worthy," Brynn said. "If I can bear the burden it represents."

"That's a lot of pressure for one person," Kira observed.

"Which is why she's not alone," Thomas said firmly. "We're all in this together."

Kira looked at each of them in turn, her expression thoughtful. "You really believe in this, don't you? All of you. It's not just a treasure hunt or an adventure. You actually think this crown exists and that finding it matters."

"It does matter," Lucian said. "The balance the crown maintains isn't abstract. When it's disrupted, bad things happen. The Shadow Wars that Lyra Stormblade fought in—those were the result of the balance breaking down. Entire kingdoms destroyed, thousands dead. If the crown is found by the wrong person, or if it's not found at all..."

"The balance tips again," Kira finished. "And history repeats itself."

"Exactly," Brynn said.

Kira pulled her knees up to her chest, wrapping her arms around them. "Then I guess it's a good thing I joined you. You clearly need all the help you can get, especially if one of you is going to keep falling in rivers."

The tension broke slightly at that, everyone managing at least a small smile.

They arranged their watch schedule—Kira volunteered for first watch, followed by Lucian, then Thomas, then Brynn. As Brynn settled into her bedroll, she felt the familiar pull of exhaustion dragging her toward sleep.

But sleep wouldn't come easily. The near-drowning had shaken her more than she wanted to admit, and something else nagged at her—something about Lucian's suggestion that they split up, about the way he'd pressed the point even when she'd expressed discomfort.

You're being paranoid, she told herself. *He saved your life at the altar. He's been nothing but helpful.*

Still, the unease persisted.

She must have dozed eventually because she woke to the sound of voices—whispered but urgent. She lay still, listening.

"—don't understand what you're asking." That was Kira, her voice tight with tension.

"I'm asking you to trust me." Lucian's voice, quiet but intense. "When the time comes, you'll need to choose a side. I'm telling you now which side is the right one."

"And if I don't agree?" Kira asked.

"Then you'll regret it," Lucian said flatly. "The crown can't fall into her hands. She's not ready. She'll fail, and the consequences will be catastrophic."

Brynn's blood ran cold. She kept her breathing steady, pretending to still be asleep while her mind raced.

"I just met these people," Kira said. "Why would I betray them for you?"

"Because I'm offering you something they can't," Lucian replied. "Power. Real power. Help me, and when I claim the crown, you'll have a place at my side. Wealth, influence, everything you've been searching for."

"I thought you said the crown was dangerous," Kira said. "That it shouldn't fall into the wrong hands."

"Brynn is the wrong hands," Lucian said. "She's naive, untested. I've been studying the crown for twenty years, Kira. I know what it requires, what it demands. I'm the one who should claim it."

There was a long pause. Then Kira spoke, her voice carefully neutral. "I need to think about this."

"Don't think too long," Lucian warned. "We're getting close to the Fang Mountains. The second trial will be there, and that's when I'll need your help. When I'll need you to make sure Brynn doesn't reach the crown before I do."

Footsteps moved away—Lucian returning to his bedroll. Brynn heard Kira take a shaky breath, then the sound of her settling back into her watch position.

Brynn's mind spun. Lucian had been lying to them. His tragic story about his family, his remorse about using magic—had any of it been true? Or had he been manipulating them from the beginning, positioning himself to steal the crown when they got close enough?

She wanted to wake Thomas immediately, to tell him what she'd heard. But something stopped her. If she confronted Lucian now, in the middle of nowhere, it could turn violent. And she didn't know where Kira stood—would the translator side with Lucian for the promised rewards, or could she be trusted?

Wait, Brynn decided. *Watch. Listen. Gather information before acting.*

It was the hardest decision she'd made since finding the map, but she forced herself to lie still, to breathe steadily, to pretend sleep while her heart hammered against her ribs.

When Thomas woke her for her watch several hours later, she took her position by the fire and waited until she was sure both Lucian and Kira were asleep. Then she moved to Thomas's bedroll and gently shook him awake.

"What's wrong?" he whispered immediately, reading something in her expression.

"We need to talk," Brynn whispered back. "Quietly. Come with me."

They moved to the far edge of the cave, where the sound of rain would cover their voices. Brynn told Thomas everything she'd overheard, watching his expression shift from confusion to shock to cold anger.

"That bastard," Thomas said quietly. "He's been planning this from the beginning?"

"I don't know," Brynn admitted. "Maybe. Or maybe he decided along the way that he wanted the crown for himself. But either way, we can't trust him anymore."

"What about Kira?" Thomas asked. "Do we trust her?"

"I don't know," Brynn said. "She didn't agree to help him, but she didn't refuse either. She said she needed to think about it."

"So we trust no one," Thomas said grimly.

"We trust each other," Brynn corrected. "And we stay alert. Watch them both. But we can't let on that we know. If Lucian realizes we've discovered his plan, he might act before we're ready."

"When do we make our move?" Thomas asked.

"When we reach the second trial," Brynn said. "Lucian said that's when he needs Kira's help to stop me from reaching the crown. So that's when we'll be ready for him."

Thomas nodded slowly. "This is going to be dangerous."

"Everything about this quest has been dangerous," Brynn pointed out. "But at least now we know where the real danger is coming from."

They returned to their positions, and Brynn finished her watch alone, staring into the fire and thinking about trust and betrayal, about the second trial that supposedly tested bonds between people.

Maybe the trial isn't about forming bonds, she thought. *Maybe it's about knowing which bonds to break.*

Dawn came gray and cold, the rain having stopped but leaving everything damp and miserable. They broke camp in tense silence that Lucian seemed to attribute to the weather and lack of sleep.

"We should reach the foothills of the Fang Mountains by tonight," he said, consulting his leather map. "Tomorrow we'll begin the climb."

"And the second trial?" Brynn asked, keeping her voice neutral. "Do you know where it is?"

Lucian glanced at her sharply, but her expression remained innocently curious. "Somewhere in the mountains," he said. "The exact location isn't marked. We'll know it when we see it."

Yes, Brynn thought grimly. *I'm sure you will.*

They set off into the damp forest, four travelers moving toward the mountains that rose like jagged teeth against the northern sky.

But now, instead of being united in purpose, they were divided by secrets and lies.

And Brynn knew that before they reached the crown, before the quest could end, they would have to face not just magical trials and physical dangers, but the worst threat of all—the enemy within their own group.

The second trial was coming.

And it would test them in ways the altar never had.

Chapter 7: The Fang Mountains

The Fang Mountains earned their name.

From a distance, they'd looked merely impressive—tall peaks, snow-capped and imposing. But up close, Brynn understood why travelers spoke of them with fear. The mountains rose in sharp, irregular spires that looked less like natural formations and more like enormous teeth thrust up from the earth's jaw. The stone itself was dark—almost black in places—and seemed to absorb light rather than reflect it.

They reached the foothills as the sun was setting, painting the jagged peaks in shades of blood-red and deep purple that made them look even more ominous.

"We'll camp here tonight," Lucian said, gesturing to a sheltered spot among large boulders. "Tomorrow we begin the ascent in earnest."

"How long to cross the mountains?" Kira asked, eyeing the peaks with obvious trepidation.

"Three days, if the weather holds and we don't encounter trouble," Lucian said. "Five or six if we're unlucky."

"Define trouble," Thomas said.

"Rockslides. Sudden storms. Ice on the paths. Creatures that live in high places and don't like visitors." Lucian smiled, but there was no humor in it. "The usual mountain hazards, but worse. These peaks have a reputation for being hostile to travelers."

Brynn exchanged a quick glance with Thomas. Since overhearing Lucian's conversation with Kira two nights ago, they'd been carefully maintaining the appearance of trust while watching both their companions closely. So far, neither Lucian nor Kira had done anything overtly suspicious, but the tension between the four of them had grown thick enough to cut.

They made camp with practiced efficiency, though Brynn noticed that Thomas positioned his bedroll closer to hers than usual, and when Lucian offered to take first watch, Thomas quickly volunteered to join him.

"Two watchers in these mountains makes sense," Thomas said casually. "More dangerous here than in the lowlands."

Lucian's eyes narrowed slightly, but he agreed. "If you insist."

As Brynn settled into her bedroll, Kira moved to lie beside her. "Can we talk?" Kira whispered, so quietly that only Brynn could hear.

Brynn's body tensed. Was this when Kira would reveal her allegiance? "About what?" she whispered back.

"About Lucian," Kira said. "I need you to know something. That night when he talked to me during my watch—I know you were awake. I could tell by your breathing."

Brynn said nothing, waiting.

"I haven't given him an answer," Kira continued. "And I won't. What he's planning is wrong. But I also don't want him to know I've chosen to stand with you, because if he thinks I'm still undecided, maybe I can learn more about his plans."

"How do I know you're telling the truth?" Brynn whispered. "How do I know this isn't just another manipulation?"

"You don't," Kira admitted. "But I'm telling you anyway, because when things get bad—and they will get bad, probably at this second trial he keeps mentioning—I want you to know which side I'm on. I'm with you, Brynn. With you and Thomas."

Brynn studied Kira's face in the dim firelight, trying to read truth or deception in her expression. Finally, she nodded slightly. "Alright. But if you're lying—"

"I'm not," Kira interrupted. "I've spent my whole life trading and traveling, watching people betray each other for profit. I'm tired of it. When you talked about the crown, about balance and responsibility, it resonated with something I'd been missing. I want to be part of something that matters, not just another transaction where everyone's looking for their cut."

"Then help us," Brynn said. "Find out what Lucian's planning. When he wants to make his move. What the second trial actually is."

"I'll try," Kira promised. "But be careful. He's dangerous, Brynn. Whatever his story about his family—true or not—he's spent twenty years studying the crown, planning for this. He won't give up easily."

They fell silent as Lucian glanced their direction, then pretended to sleep. But Brynn's mind raced. If Kira was telling the truth, they had an ally. If she was lying, they were walking into a trap.

Either way, the confrontation was coming.

Dawn broke cold and gray. They ate a quick breakfast of dried fruit and the last of their bread, then began the climb into the Fang Mountains proper.

The path—if it could be called that—was treacherous from the start. Loose scree covered the lower slopes, shifting dangerously underfoot. The higher they climbed, the steeper it became, until they were scrambling over rocks with their hands as much as their feet.

"There," Lucian said around midmorning, pointing to a narrow cleft between two massive spires. "That's our route through. It's the only pass for twenty miles in either direction that doesn't require actual climbing equipment."

The cleft was perhaps ten feet wide at its base, narrowing to barely six feet at the top. The walls on either side rose hundreds of feet, dark stone that seemed to lean inward, creating a claustrophobic tunnel through the mountain's heart.

"I don't like it," Thomas said immediately. "Too easy to be trapped in there."

"Which is why I'll go first," Lucian said. "Scout ahead, make sure it's clear. Give me thirty minutes. If I don't return or signal, find another route."

Before anyone could argue, he entered the cleft and disappeared into shadow.

"We're not waiting thirty minutes," Thomas said quietly as soon as Lucian was out of earshot. "This could be his move. He could be setting up an ambush in there right now."

"Or he could actually be scouting," Kira pointed out. "We can't assume everything he does is hostile."

"Can't we?" Thomas asked sharply.

"Enough," Brynn said. "We give him fifteen minutes. Then we follow, but we go prepared for trouble."

They spent the fifteen minutes checking weapons and positioning themselves for a quick entry into the cleft if needed. Brynn pulled out the map, studying it in the morning light.

The parchment showed the mountains in detail, with the pass marked clearly. But there was something else—a symbol she hadn't noticed before, glowing faintly just beyond the pass. It looked like the same symbol that had marked the altar.

"The second trial," she breathed. "It's just beyond this pass. That's why Lucian wanted to scout ahead—he's looking for it."

"Then we go now," Thomas said. "Before he finds it without us."

They entered the cleft cautiously, weapons drawn. The passage was exactly as claustrophobic as it had looked from outside—narrow walls of dark stone rising on either side, the path winding slightly so they couldn't see more than twenty feet ahead. Their footsteps echoed strangely, and the temperature dropped noticeably, the stone seeming to radiate cold.

They'd gone perhaps a hundred yards when they heard it—a sound like stone scraping against stone, and then Lucian's voice, strained with effort: "Help! I need help!"

Thomas started to rush forward, but Brynn grabbed his arm. "Wait," she said quietly. "It could be a trap."

"Or he could actually need help," Kira said. "If he's hurt and we left him—"

Another sound—definitely stone moving, and then a crash that shook the entire passage. Dust rained down from above.

"Rockslide," Thomas said. "Real or manufactured, we need to move. This whole passage could collapse."

They ran forward, rounding a bend to find Lucian pinned beneath a large boulder that had fallen from above. His staff lay just out of reach, and his face was twisted with pain.

"Help me," he gasped. "My leg—I think it's broken."

Thomas and Brynn exchanged glances. This could be genuine. It could also be the perfect setup —all of them occupied trying to free Lucian while he struck at them.

"Kira, watch our backs," Brynn ordered. "Thomas, help me with this rock."

They positioned themselves on either side of the boulder, finding handholds on its rough surface. On three, they heaved, and the rock shifted slightly. Lucian cried out as the movement jostled his trapped leg.

"Again," Thomas said, and they lifted once more.

This time the boulder shifted enough that Lucian could pull his leg free. He scrambled back, gasping, his face pale. His left leg was bent at an unnatural angle below the knee.

"Definitely broken," Kira said, kneeling to examine it. "I can splint it, but he won't be walking on it for weeks."

"We don't have weeks," Lucian said through gritted teeth. "The trial is close. I can feel it. You'll have to go on without me."

"That's convenient," Thomas said flatly. "We leave you here, you wait until we're past, then somehow your leg isn't as broken as it looked and you follow to steal the crown."

Lucian's expression hardened. "You know."

"We know," Brynn confirmed. "We heard you talking to Kira. We know you want the crown for yourself."

Lucian laughed—a bitter, pained sound. "Of course you did. I should have been more careful." He looked at each of them in turn. "But you don't understand. I'm not the villain here. I'm trying to prevent a disaster."

"By lying to us?" Thomas demanded. "By planning to betray us?"

"By doing what's necessary," Lucian said. "Brynn is not ready for the crown's burden. I've seen it before—young, idealistic seekers who think they can wield such power responsibly. They all fail. They all either break under the weight or become corrupted by it."

"And you're different?" Brynn asked.

"I've studied the crown for twenty years," Lucian said. "I know its history, its requirements, its dangers. I've prepared myself for this burden in ways you can't imagine. My story about my family— that was true. I did destroy them with uncontrolled magic. But I've spent two decades learning control, learning discipline, learning how to wield power without being consumed by it."

"Or learning how to justify taking what isn't yours," Kira said quietly.

Lucian's eyes flashed. "You dare judge me? You, who spend your life helping merchants exploit price differences between desperate people? At least I've been working toward something meaningful."

"Enough," Brynn said. "You're right about one thing—I'm not sure I'm ready for the crown's burden. But I'm called to it, Lucian. The map chose me. The altar confirmed me. Whether I feel ready or not, this is my path. Not yours."

"Then you'll fail," Lucian said flatly. "And when you do, the balance will tip again. The Shadow Wars will return. Thousands will die. All because you were too proud to step aside for someone better prepared."

"Or," Brynn said, "I'll succeed. And you'll be the one who has to live with trying to steal a destiny that was never meant for you."

She turned to Thomas and Kira. "We leave him here. Splint his leg so he doesn't die, but we're not taking him with us."

"You can't leave me," Lucian said, desperation creeping into his voice. "In these mountains, injured, I'll die. Exposure, thirst, or something worse will find me."

"You have your staff," Brynn said coldly. "Use your magic to protect yourself. The same magic you said you'd never use again but clearly have no problem wielding when it suits you."

Kira worked quickly to splint Lucian's leg using branches Thomas gathered from stunted pines growing between rocks. Lucian didn't speak again, just watched them with eyes full of barely suppressed rage.

"I underestimated you," he finally said as they prepared to leave. "All of you. But especially you, Brynn. Your grandmother would be proud—you have her ruthlessness when necessary."

"My grandmother would be disappointed in you," Brynn replied. "She came to this altar, saw you in the mountains, and still chose to walk away. Because she understood something you don't—the crown isn't about power or worthiness. It's about purpose. About being willing to serve rather than rule."

She turned away from him and walked deeper into the pass, Thomas and Kira following. Behind them, Lucian called out one last time: "You haven't seen the last of me! I'll reach that crown, one way or another!"

His voice echoed off the stone walls, following them like a curse.

They emerged from the cleft into a hidden valley that took Brynn's breath away. It was circular, perhaps a mile across, ringed by the sharp peaks of the Fang Mountains. But inside the ring, the landscape was impossibly green and lush—grass, flowers, even trees growing where no vegetation should exist at this altitude.

And in the center of the valley, rising from a pool of crystal-clear water, was a structure that could only be the second trial.

It was a bridge—delicate, made of what looked like glass or crystal, arching over the water in a graceful curve. But the bridge led nowhere—it simply arced up from one side of the pool, reached its apex perhaps fifty feet in the air, then descended back to the same shore it had started from.

A bridge that led nowhere. A journey that ended where it began.

"What kind of trial is this?" Thomas asked, staring at the impossible structure.

Brynn pulled out the map. The symbol here glowed brilliantly, pulsing in time with her heartbeat. And as she watched, words appeared on the parchment—words that hadn't been there before:

The second trial tests not the seeker, but those who walk beside them. Trust is the bridge. Faith is the path. Only together can you cross what cannot be crossed alone.

"It's not about me," Brynn said slowly, understanding dawning. "The second trial isn't testing me at all. It's testing all of us. Testing whether we can truly trust each other enough to do something impossible."

She looked at Thomas and Kira, these two people who'd followed her into danger, who'd stayed beside her even when they learned the true stakes.

"We have to walk that bridge," she said. "Together. And somehow, it will take us where we need to go. But only if we trust each other completely."

Thomas stepped forward without hesitation. "Then let's walk."

Kira hesitated only a moment before joining him. "I'm with you. Whatever comes next."

The three of them approached the bridge, the crystal structure gleaming in the mountain sunlight. And as they placed their feet on its impossible surface, the true test began.

Chapter 8: The Bridge Of Trust

The crystal bridge felt solid beneath Brynn's feet, which somehow made it more unsettling rather than less. Something that looked so delicate, so impossible, shouldn't feel stable. Yet each step she took produced a faint chime, like walking on musical glass, and the surface held her weight without flexing or cracking.

Thomas walked beside her on her right, and Kira on her left. They'd agreed without speaking to stay close together, their shoulders nearly touching as they climbed the bridge's upward arc.

"It's beautiful," Kira said softly, looking down at the pool beneath them. The water was so clear they could see every pebble on the bottom, and fish that glowed with their own inner light swam in lazy circles.

"Don't look down too long," Thomas warned. "Height like this can make you dizzy."

They were perhaps twenty feet up now, the bridge continuing its graceful curve toward the apex fifty feet above the valley floor. Brynn could feel something building—a pressure in the air, a sense of potential energy gathering around them like a storm about to break.

"Stay together," she said, though she wasn't sure why she felt compelled to say it. "No matter what happens, stay together."

They reached the bridge's highest point and stopped, standing at the apex of the impossible arc. From here, Brynn could see the entire hidden valley—the ring of mountains, the lush impossible vegetation, and in the distance, a silver line that might have been the river they'd been following.

"Now what?" Thomas asked. "The bridge just curves back down to where we started. There's nowhere to—"

The world shifted.

One moment they were standing on the crystal bridge in bright sunlight. The next, darkness enveloped them—not the darkness of night but something deeper, more profound. A darkness that felt alive, watching, testing.

Brynn reached out instinctively and felt Thomas's hand grab hers on one side, Kira's on the other. The three of them stood in the void, holding onto each other like anchors in a storm.

The second trial begins, a voice said—not the same voice from the altar, but similar in its otherworldly quality. *You who seek the crown must prove you understand its first principle: no guardian stands alone. Power shared is power multiplied. Trust given is strength gained.*

"What do you want us to do?" Brynn called into the darkness.

Walk forward, the voice replied. *But know this—the path ahead shows each of you your deepest fear. See them. Face them. Support each other through them. Only by carrying one another's burdens can you proceed.*

Light began to filter back, but it was wrong somehow—dim and sickly, casting strange shadows. Brynn found they were still on the bridge, but the valley below had changed. It was no longer beautiful and lush but dead, twisted, corrupted.

And then she saw it.

Her grandmother stood at the end of the bridge, exactly as Brynn remembered her from the week before she died—frail, diminished by illness, but with eyes still sharp and aware.

"Brynn," Aubre said, her voice weak. "You've failed me. The crown is lost. Everything I sacrificed, everything I waited for—wasted because you weren't strong enough."

Brynn's breath caught. She knew this wasn't real, knew it was the trial testing her, but the words cut deep anyway. "No," she said, her voice shaking. "That's not true."

"Isn't it?" Her grandmother's image smiled sadly. "I gave up my destiny for you. I lived an ordinary life, married, raised a family, all because I believed you would be the one to claim what I could not. And you've proven me wrong. The crown will fall to someone like Lucian—someone hungry for power, someone who will corrupt its purpose. And it will be your fault."

Tears blurred Brynn's vision. The accusation struck at her deepest fear—that she wasn't worthy of the calling, that her grandmother's sacrifice had been wasted on someone too weak, too uncertain, too flawed.

"Brynn." Thomas's voice, firm and steady beside her. "That's not your grandmother. Your grandmother believed in you. She wouldn't say these things."

"She trusted you," Kira added from her other side. "She prepared you. That's what you told us, remember? Every story, every lesson—she was getting you ready. She knew you could do this."

Brynn took a shaking breath and looked directly at the image of her grandmother. "You're right that Grandmother believed in me. Which is exactly why I know you're not her. She would never tear me down like this. She would lift me up, even when I doubted myself."

The image wavered, then dissolved like smoke. The bridge ahead cleared slightly, and they took several steps forward.

"That was yours," Thomas said quietly to Brynn. "Now comes mine."

The light shifted again, and suddenly they were standing in the ruins of Thornhaven. Buildings burned, bodies lay in the streets, and the forge where Thomas had worked his entire life was nothing but smoking rubble.

A figure emerged from the destruction—Thomas's father, his face blackened with soot and twisted with rage.

"You left," the image said, pointing an accusing finger at Thomas. "You abandoned us for this fool's quest. And while you were gone, they came. The shadow forces that the crown was supposed to keep at bay—they came because the balance was broken. Because Brynn failed. Because you weren't here to protect us."

Thomas went rigid beside Brynn, his hand tightening painfully around hers. "Father," he whispered.

"I'm not your father anymore," the image spat. "You're no son of mine. A real son would have stayed, would have protected his family and his home. But you threw it all away for a girl who was never going to succeed anyway."

Brynn felt Thomas shaking, felt the weight of his guilt and fear. She understood now—Thomas's deepest terror wasn't about his own failure but about failing those he'd left behind.

"Thomas," she said firmly. "Look at me. Look at me, not at him."

Thomas tore his gaze away from his father's image and looked at Brynn.

"Your father is safe in Thornhaven," Brynn said. "This hasn't happened. This is just fear—your fear that leaving was selfish, that you abandoned your responsibilities. But you didn't. You chose to help prevent something worse. To help maintain the balance so that what this vision shows never happens."

"She's right," Kira said. "You're not running away from responsibility. You're facing a greater one. That takes courage, not cowardice."

Thomas nodded slowly, his jaw set. He turned back to the image of his father. "You taught me to do what's right, even when it's hard," he said. "Even when it costs us. This is me doing what's right. And I know—I know—that the real you would understand that."

The image flickered and vanished. The burning ruins of Thornhaven faded, and the bridge stretched forward once more. They walked together, and after a dozen steps, the light shifted a third time.

"My turn," Kira said quietly, her voice tight with anticipation and dread.

The scene that materialized around them was different from the others—not apocalyptic or accusatory but intimate. They stood in what looked like a comfortable home—modest but well-kept, with signs of family life everywhere. Children's drawings on the walls. Books on shelves. A fire crackling in a hearth.

And standing in the center of it all was Kira herself—or rather, another version of her. This Kira looked settled, content, wearing simple clothes and a wedding ring. Beside her stood a man whose face was kind, and at her feet played two small children.

"This is what you gave up," the domestic Kira said, and her voice held no accusation, only sadness. "This is the life you could have had if you'd made different choices. If you'd stopped traveling, stopped searching for meaning in distant places. If you'd just settled down somewhere and built something real."

The Kira beside Brynn made a small sound—something between a gasp and a sob.

"You're always moving," the image continued. "Always looking for the next thing, the next place, the next adventure. But what are you running from, Kira? What are you afraid to face?"

"I'm not running," Kira said, but her voice lacked conviction.

"Aren't you?" The domestic Kira gestured to the peaceful scene. "You say you want meaning, want to be part of something important. But maybe that's just an excuse. Maybe you're afraid that if you stop moving, you'll have to confront the fact that you don't know who you are. That you've spent so long being whoever merchants and travelers needed you to be that you've lost yourself."

Kira was shaking now, and Brynn squeezed her hand tighter. "Kira," she said gently. "Is this true? Is this what you fear?"

"I don't know who I am," Kira admitted, tears streaming down her face. "I speak six languages but I've forgotten which one I dreamed in as a child. I've been to fifty cities but I can't remember which one was home. I've translated a thousand conversations but I can't remember the last time I said something that was genuinely, completely, only mine."

"Then find out," Thomas said firmly. "Not by settling for a life that looks safe but by doing something that matters. By being part of this quest. By choosing to help us not because someone's paying you or because it's convenient, but because it's right."

"You're not running," Brynn added. "You're searching. And maybe what you're searching for isn't a place or a purpose but yourself. The real you, underneath all the languages and personas. And maybe—maybe the way you find that is by standing with us. By making a choice that's completely yours."

Kira looked at the domestic scene—the peaceful life, the family, the stability. Then she looked at Brynn and Thomas—her companions on this impossible journey.

"I choose this," Kira said firmly, addressing the image. "I choose the quest, the danger, the uncertainty. Not because I'm running from you, but because I'm running toward something. Toward meaning. Toward truth. Toward becoming who I'm supposed to be instead of just existing as what others need."

The domestic scene shimmered and faded. The three of them stood alone on the bridge once more, but the darkness was lifting. The valley below was returning to its beautiful, lush state.

You have passed the second trial, the voice said, and now it sounded almost warm, almost proud. *You have faced your fears and supported each other through them. You have proven that trust is stronger than terror, that bonds freely chosen can bear any weight.*

The bridge beneath them began to glow, light rising from the crystal structure and enveloping them in warmth. Brynn felt something settling into her chest—not just relief but a deeper certainty. She wasn't alone in this quest. She had true companions, people who would stand with her not from obligation but from genuine connection.

Walk forward, the voice instructed. *Walk together. And see where the bridge that led nowhere can take those who trust completely.*

They walked down the descending arc of the bridge, hands still linked. But when they reached what should have been the same shore they'd started from, everything had changed.

The pool was gone. The lush valley was gone. Instead, they stood at the edge of a vast canyon, with a silver river flowing far below. And spanning the canyon was a real bridge—solid stone, ancient and weathered but clearly functional.

On the far side of the canyon, perhaps a mile distant, Brynn could see their destination—a valley that seemed to shine with its own light, nestled between peaks that looked less like teeth and more like guardian pillars.

The Crystal Valley. Where the Crimson Crown waited.

"We did it," Thomas said, wonder in his voice. "The impossible bridge brought us... here. Across miles. Across the mountains themselves."

"Because we trusted each other," Kira said softly. "Because we faced our fears together."

"And because we're stronger together than any of us could be alone," Brynn finished. She looked at her companions—her friends. "Whatever comes next, whatever final trial awaits us, we face it as we've faced everything else. Together."

They crossed the stone bridge, their footsteps echoing in the canyon below. As they reached the far side and stood at the entrance to the Crystal Valley, Brynn felt the map pulse against her chest, felt the crown's presence like a beacon.

The second trial was complete.

The crown was close now. So close.

But first, they would have to deal with one more obstacle—because as they stood at the valley's entrance, a figure emerged from the shadows ahead, leaning heavily on a staff.

Lucian.

His leg was still splinted, his face was drawn with pain and exhaustion, but his eyes burned with determination and something darker—desperation.

"I told you," he said, his voice rough. "You haven't seen the last of me."

Behind him, the Crystal Valley waited, luminous and promising and just out of reach.

The final confrontation had arrived.

Chapter 9: The Final Guardian

Lucian looked like death walking.

His splinted leg dragged behind him, leaving a trail in the crystalline sand that covered the valley's entrance. His face was gray with exhaustion and pain, his clothes torn and stained. But his eyes—his eyes burned with an intensity that made Brynn's hand drift toward her knife.

"How did you get here?" Thomas demanded, stepping forward protectively. "Your leg was broken. You were miles behind us."

"Magic," Lucian said simply, leaning heavily on his staff. "The same magic I swore never to use again. The same magic that cost me my family." He laughed bitterly. "But what's one more broken vow when the crown is at stake?"

"You can barely stand," Kira observed. "Whatever magic you used, it's killing you. Look at yourself, Lucian. You're dying."

"Perhaps," Lucian admitted. "Magic always demands payment, and I've made quite a withdrawal these past hours. But I'll live long enough to do what must be done."

"Which is what?" Brynn asked, keeping her voice steady despite the fear coiling in her stomach. "Stop me from reaching the crown? Kill us?"

"Stop you, yes. Kill you?" Lucian shook his head. "I'm not a murderer, Brynn. I'm just someone who's spent twenty years preparing for this moment while you've had twenty days. The crown requires knowledge, discipline, understanding that you simply don't possess."

"The crown requires a pure heart," Brynn countered. "Not knowledge or power. That's what every guardian has taught, from the Celestial Smiths onward. You've studied the crown's history but learned nothing from it."

Lucian's expression darkened. "Don't lecture me about the crown's requirements. I know more about it than you ever will. I know its weight, its burden, it's terrible responsibility. And I know you'll break under it."

"Then you don't know me at all," Brynn said.

"I know enough. I know you're barely more than a girl playing at being a hero. I know you've been lucky so far—lucky in your companions, lucky in your timing, lucky that I underestimated you."

Lucian straightened as much as his injured leg allowed. "But your luck ends here. I'm invoking the right of challenge."

The words hung in the air like a pronouncement of doom. Thomas moved closer to Brynn, his hand on his sword. Kira tensed, ready to act.

"What right of challenge?" Brynn asked, though something in her grandmother's journal had mentioned this, buried in the sections she hadn't fully absorbed.

"Ancient law," Lucian said. "When two seekers reach the crown's final guardian at the same time, either may challenge the other. The guardian decides between them—tests them, judges them, determines who is worthy and who is not."

"Final guardian?" Thomas looked around the apparently empty valley. "There's no one here but us."

As if in response to his words, the ground beneath them began to tremble. The crystalline sand rose in a whirlwind, coalescing into a form—first vague and shapeless, then gradually taking definition.

It solidified into a figure that stood perhaps twelve feet tall, vaguely humanoid but clearly not human. Its body seemed to be made of the same crystal as the bridge they'd crossed, translucent and glowing from within. Where its face should be, there was only a smooth surface that somehow suggested awareness, judgment, wisdom beyond mortal comprehension.

I am the Keeper, a voice said—not spoken aloud but felt in Brynn's bones, resonating through her entire being. *I am the final guardian before the crown. I have stood watch since Lyra Stormblade hid it here, waiting for one worthy to claim it.*

The crystal figure turned its featureless face toward Lucian. *You invoke the ancient challenge. Do you understand what this means?*

"I do," Lucian said, his voice steady despite his obvious pain. "Two seekers. One crown. You must judge between us and determine who is worthy."

And you, the Keeper turned to Brynn. *Do you accept this challenge?*

Brynn wanted to refuse. The idea of being judged against Lucian—a man who'd spent twenty years studying the crown while she'd had mere weeks—seemed impossible to win. But she also knew refusing wasn't an option.

"I accept," she said.

Then let the challenge begin, the Keeper announced. *But know this—the challenge is not combat. The crown does not reward violence or strength of arms. The challenge is truth.*

The Keeper raised one crystalline hand, and the world shifted again—not as dramatically as the bridge trial, but subtly, like reality adjusting its focus. Brynn found herself standing in a circle of light with Lucian across from her. Thomas and Kira stood outside the circle, able to watch but not intervene.

Each of you will answer three questions, the Keeper said. *Answer truly, from your deepest self, hiding nothing. I will see through deception, through self-deception, through the lies we tell ourselves to make our choices bearable. Only absolute truth will suffice.*

"And whoever answers best is deemed worthy?" Lucian asked.

Not best. Most truly. The crown does not seek perfection. It seeks authenticity.

The Keeper turned its attention to Lucian first. *Why do you seek the crown?*

Lucian took a deep breath. "I seek it to prevent catastrophe. I've studied the Shadow Wars, the last time the balance failed. Hundreds of thousands died. Kingdoms fell. And it happened because the guardian of that time was unworthy—too weak to bear the burden, too naive to understand the stakes. I won't let history repeat itself."

That is your stated reason, the Keeper said. *Now tell the truth beneath the reason.*

Lucian's jaw tightened. For a long moment, he said nothing. Then, slowly, words emerged as if dragged from him against his will: "I seek it because I'm alone. Because I destroyed my family and spent twenty years in isolation, and the crown is the only thing that gives my suffering meaning. If I claim it, then everything I've endured, everything I've sacrificed, will have been for a purpose. I'll be more than just a man who lost control and murdered those he loved. I'll be a guardian. I'll matter."

The admission clearly cost him. His face twisted with shame and anger at having been forced to speak it aloud.

The Keeper turned to Brynn. *Why do you seek the crown?*

"Because I was called," Brynn said immediately. "Because my grandmother prepared me for this, because the map chose me, because—" She stopped, feeling the Keeper's attention like a weight. "Because I want to finish what my father started, what my grandmother couldn't. Because I want to prove I'm worthy of their faith in me."

And the truth beneath?

Brynn closed her eyes, looking inward. "Because I'm tired of being ordinary. Because I've always felt like I was meant for something more, something important, and the crown is proof that feeling wasn't just arrogance or delusion. Because claiming it means I matter. That my life has meaning beyond just existing."

She opened her eyes and found herself meeting Lucian's gaze. They'd given essentially the same answer—both seeking the crown to validate their suffering, to prove their lives mattered.

The first truth is spoken, the Keeper said. *Now the second question. What will you sacrifice to bear the crown's burden?*

"Everything," Lucian said immediately. "I've already proven that. I've given up magic, family, normal human connection. I've spent two decades preparing myself, disciplining myself, learning to control the power that once controlled me. I'll sacrifice whatever else is required."

You speak of past sacrifices, the Keeper said. *I ask about future ones. The crown does not reward what you have already lost. It demands what you still hold dear. So I ask again—what will you sacrifice?*

Lucian was silent longer this time. "My solitude," he finally said, the words bitter. "My isolation. The crown's guardian cannot stand alone— you've made that clear through the trials. I'll have to trust others again, work with them, risk caring about them. Risk losing them as I lost my family."

The Keeper turned to Brynn. *And you? What will you sacrifice?*

"My certainty," Brynn said after a moment's thought. "The belief that I know the right answer, the right path. Being a guardian means making impossible choices where every option costs something. It means accepting that I'll make mistakes, that people will suffer because of my decisions, and I'll have to live with that."

She looked at Thomas and Kira outside the circle. "It means understanding that I can't protect everyone I care about. That I might have to make choices that hurt them or put them at risk for the greater balance. And I'll have to be strong enough to make those choices anyway."

The second truth is spoken, the Keeper acknowledged. *Now the final question, and the most important. What do you fear most about claiming the crown?*

"That I'll fail," Lucian said without hesitation. "That despite all my preparation, all my study, all my sacrifice, I'll still prove unworthy. That the crown will reject me, or that I'll claim it but still be unable to prevent the disasters I've spent twenty years dreading. That everything I've done, everyone I've lost, will have been for nothing."

And you? The Keeper asked Brynn.

"That I'll succeed," Brynn said quietly.

Lucian's head snapped toward her in surprise. Even Thomas and Kira looked shocked.

"Explain," the Keeper commanded.

"If I fail," Brynn said slowly, working through the thought even as she spoke it, "then it's done. The burden passes to someone else. My responsibility ends. But if I succeed—if I claim the crown and become its guardian—then the burden never ends. Every day for the rest of my life, I'll carry that weight. I'll make decisions that affect thousands, maybe millions. I'll have to balance competing goods, choose between terrible options, live with the consequences of my choices."

She took a shaky breath. "Failure would be painful but brief. Success means a lifetime of pain, of doubt, of being responsible for things I can't fully control. And I'm terrified that I'll spend that lifetime wondering if Lucian was right—if I'm too young, too inexperienced, too naive. If every mistake I make could have been avoided by someone wiser, someone better prepared."

"Then step aside," Lucian said urgently. "Let me take that burden. You don't want it—you just said so. Let me carry what I've been preparing to carry for twenty years."

"No," Brynn said. "Because wanting it or not wanting it isn't what matters. You're right that I'm terrified of success. But I'm more terrified of failing those who believed in me. Of wasting my grandmother's sacrifice. Of letting the balance tip because I was too afraid to accept my calling."

She met the Keeper's featureless face. "I don't want the crown's burden. But I accept it anyway. Not because I'm eager for power or confident I won't fail, but because it's mine to carry whether I want it or not. That's the difference between Lucian and me—he wants to earn worthiness through preparation. I'm accepting that worthiness isn't something you earn. It's something you're called to, ready or not."

The Keeper was silent for a long moment, its crystalline form pulsing with inner light. Then it spoke, its voice resonating with finality:

The challenge is complete. The truth has been spoken by both seekers. And my judgment is rendered.

The crystal figure turned fully toward Lucian. *You seek the crown to heal yourself, to make meaning from suffering. This is not wrong, but it is not sufficient. The crown's guardian must serve the balance, not their own need for redemption. You have spent twenty years preparing your mind and power, but you have not prepared your heart. You remain broken, and you seek the crown to make yourself whole. This is the wrong order.*

Lucian's face crumpled. "No. No, I've given everything—"

You have given much, the Keeper acknowledged. *But you have given it to yourself, not to the balance. Your service would be tainted by your need. I am sorry, seeker. You are not the one.*

The circle of light around Lucian faded, and he stumbled back, catching himself on his staff. He looked at Brynn with eyes full of anguish and rage and something that might have been relief.

The Keeper turned to Brynn. *You fear success more than failure. You doubt your worthiness. You acknowledge your inexperience and limitations. These should be weaknesses, yet they are your greatest strengths.*

The crystal figure raised both hands, and the light around Brynn intensified. *You do not seek the crown to heal yourself or prove your worth. You seek it because you were called, and you accept that calling despite your fears. You understand that the guardian serves the balance, not themselves. You know you will make mistakes, and you will bear that knowledge with humility rather than arrogance.*

Most importantly, you understand that the guardian does not stand alone. You have proven this through the trials—you trust your companions, you accept their support, you share the burden rather than hoarding it. This is what makes a true guardian.

The Keeper's voice seemed to fill the entire valley. *Brynn Thornwick, granddaughter of Meredith, I name you worthy. The crown awaits. Go and claim what is yours.*

The circle of light faded, and Brynn found herself standing in the valley once more, Thomas and Kira rushing to her side.

"You did it," Thomas said, his voice full of wonder. "The Keeper chose you."

"Not chose," Brynn corrected. "Confirmed. The choice was made long ago." She looked at Lucian, who stood apart, his face a mask of conflicting emotions. "I'm sorry," she said to him. "I know this isn't what you wanted."

"Sorry?" Lucian laughed—a broken sound. "You have nothing to apologize for. The Keeper was right. I sought the crown for the wrong reasons, and some part of me knew it all along." He looked at her, and his expression softened slightly. "My grandmother saw you in her vision. She knew, even twenty years ago, that you would be the one. Not me."

"What will you do now?" Kira asked him.

Lucian glanced at his splinted leg, then at the valley around them. "Rest, I suppose. Heal. Think about what the Keeper said about my heart not being prepared." He met Brynn's eyes. "I won't try to stop you anymore. The challenge is complete, the judgment rendered. The crown is yours by right. But Brynn—"

"Yes?"

"Don't make my mistakes. Don't let the burden consume you. Don't think you have to carry it alone."

He gestured to Thomas and Kira. "You have something I never had—people who stand with you not because they have to, but because they choose to. Don't waste that gift."

"I won't," Brynn promised.

She turned toward the Crystal Valley proper, where somewhere among the glittering formations, the Crimson Crown waited. The final trial was complete. The judgment was rendered.

Now came the moment she'd been moving toward since finding the map in her grandmother's attic.

The moment she claimed her destiny.

Chapter 10: The Final Guardian

Lucian looked like death walking.

His splinted leg dragged behind him, leaving a trail in the crystalline sand that covered the valley's entrance. His face was gray with exhaustion and pain, his clothes torn and stained with blood. But his eyes—his eyes burned with an intensity that made Brynn's hand drift toward her knife.

"How did you get here?" Thomas demanded, stepping in front of Brynn protectively. "Your leg was broken. You were miles behind us."

"Magic," Lucian said simply, leaning heavily on his staff. The wood itself seemed darker than before, as if the power he'd channeled through it had burned away something essential. "The same magic I swore never to use again. The same magic that cost me everything."

He took another step forward, and Brynn saw him wince despite his efforts to hide it. Whatever spell he'd used to transport himself here had extracted a terrible price. Dark veins spread from beneath his sleeves, crawling up his neck like corrupted roots beneath skin.

"You're dying," Kira said quietly.

"Perhaps," Lucian admitted. "Magic always demands payment, and I've made quite a withdrawal these past hours. But I'll live long enough to do what must be done."

"Which is what?" Brynn asked, keeping her voice steady despite the fear coiling in her stomach. "Stop me from reaching the crown? Kill us?"

"Stop you, yes." Lucian's laugh was bitter. "Kill you? No, child. I'm not a murderer. I'm just someone who's spent twenty years preparing for this moment while you've had barely twenty days."

"The crown doesn't measure time in years of study," Brynn said. "It measures hearts."

"Does it?" Lucian's eyes flashed. "Is that what your grandmother told you in her stories? That heart alone is enough?" He took another painful step. "I had heart once. I had love. I had a family. And in one moment of uncontrolled power, I destroyed them all. So tell me, Brynn Thornwick:—what good is heart without the discipline to wield what you've been given?"

The words struck deeper than Brynn wanted to admit. Wasn't that exactly what she feared? That she'd claim power she couldn't control, hurt people she was trying to protect?

"Then teach her," Thomas said suddenly. Everyone turned to look at him. "If you truly believe she needs discipline, knowledge, understanding—then teach her. Help her. Be the mentor you claim she needs instead of the obstacle she has to overcome."

For a moment, something flickered across Lucian's face—surprise, perhaps, or the ghost of the man he'd been before grief had hollowed him out. Then it hardened again.

"It's too late for that," he said. "The crown calls. It's here, now, waiting. And only one of us will claim it." He planted his staff firmly. "I invoke the right of challenge."

The words hung in the air like a pronouncement of doom. The very atmosphere seemed to thicken, responding to the ancient formula.

"What right of challenge?" Brynn asked, though her grandmother's journal had mentioned this. She'd read about it in those long midnight hours by firelight, but the details had seemed like ancient history, not something that could touch her life.

"When two seekers reach the crown's final guardian at the same time," Lucian said, "either may invoke the ancient right. The guardian decides between them—tests them, judges them, determines who is worthy and who is not."

"Final guardian?" Thomas looked around the valley. "There's no one here but us."

As if his words had summoned it, the ground beneath them began to tremble.

The crystalline sand rose in a whirlwind, spiraling upward with a sound like a thousand wind chimes singing in unison. The particles spun faster, tighter, taking shape. Light gathered at the vortex's center, growing brighter until Brynn had to shield her eyes.

When the light faded and the sand settled, a figure stood before them.

It was tall—perhaps twelve feet—and vaguely humanoid but clearly not human. Its body seemed carved from the same crystal as the bridge they'd crossed, translucent and glowing from within with soft, pulsing light. Where a face should be, there was only a smooth expanse of crystal that somehow suggested vast awareness, infinite patience, and a wisdom that predated human language.

The figure's presence pressed against Brynn's mind like a weight made of music and light.

I am the Keeper, a voice said—not spoken aloud but felt in the bones, resonating through the very air. *I am the final guardian before the crown. I have stood watch since Lyra Stormblade hid it with her dying breath, waiting for one worthy to claim what she protected.*

The Keeper turned its featureless face toward Lucian, and even from several feet away, Brynn could feel the intensity of that gaze.

You invoke the ancient challenge, the Keeper said. *Do you understand what this means? Do you accept the price of your invocation?*

"I do," Lucian said, his voice steady despite his obvious pain. "Two seekers. One crown. You must judge between us and determine who is worthy."

And you? The Keeper turned to Brynn. *Do you accept this challenge?*

Brynn wanted to refuse. The idea of being judged against Lucian—a man who'd spent two decades studying the crown, preparing himself, disciplining his power—seemed impossible to win. She was a girl from a small village who'd found a map in her grandmother's attic barely a month ago.

But she also knew refusing wasn't an option. The crown had called her. Her grandmother had prepared her for this. And somehow, despite all her doubts, she'd passed every trial to reach this moment.

"I accept," she said.

Then let the challenge begin.

The Keeper raised one crystalline hand, and the world shifted. Not dramatically, like the bridge trial, but subtly—like reality adjusting its focus, sharpening certain details while softening others. Brynn found herself standing in a circle of pure white light, Lucian across from her. Thomas and Kira stood outside the circle, able to see and hear but unable to intervene.

The challenge is not combat, the Keeper said, its voice filling the circle. *The crown does not reward violence or strength of arms. The challenge is truth. Each of you will answer three questions. Answer truly, from your deepest self, hiding nothing. I will see through deception, through self-deception, through the lies we tell ourselves to make our choices bearable. Only absolute truth will suffice.*

"And whoever answers best is deemed worthy?" Lucian asked.

Not best. Most truly. The crown does not seek perfection. It seeks authenticity.

The Keeper's presence intensified, focusing on Lucian like sunlight through glass.

Why do you seek the crown?

Lucian straightened as much as his injured leg allowed. "I seek it to prevent catastrophe. I've studied the Shadow Wars, the last time the balance failed. I know what happens when the wrong person claims this power, or when no one claims it at all. Hundreds of thousands died. Kingdoms fell. Entire bloodlines were erased from existence. I won't let that happen again."

That is your stated reason, the Keeper said. *Now tell the truth beneath the reason. The truth you hide even from yourself.*

Lucian's jaw tightened. Sweat beaded on his forehead. For a long moment, he said nothing, and Brynn could see him fighting against the compulsion to speak. But the Keeper's power was inexorable.

Words emerged from Lucian's throat as if dragged out against his will: "I seek it because I'm alone. Because I destroyed my family and spent twenty years in isolation, and the crown is the only thing that gives my suffering meaning. If I claim it, then everything I've endured, everything I've sacrificed, will have been for a purpose. I'll be more than just a man who lost control and murdered those he loved. I'll be a guardian. I'll matter."

The admission clearly cost him everything. His face twisted with shame and rage at having been forced to speak his deepest truth aloud.

The Keeper turned to Brynn, and she felt that same inexorable pressure.

Why do you seek the crown?

"Because I was called," Brynn said immediately. "Because my grandmother prepared me for this, because the map chose me, because the altar confirmed me—" She stopped, feeling the Keeper's attention intensify. The being wanted more than the surface truth.

She took a breath. "Because I want to finish what my grandmother started. What she couldn't complete. I want to prove I'm worthy of her faith in me. That her sacrifice wasn't wasted."

And the truth beneath?

Brynn closed her eyes. The Keeper's power wrapped around her like gentle, implacable hands, drawing truth from depths she hadn't wanted to examine.

"Because I'm tired of being ordinary," she said quietly. "Because I've always felt like I was meant for something more, something important, and the crown is proof that feeling wasn't just arrogance or delusion. Because claiming it means I matter. That my life has meaning beyond just existing in Thornhaven until I die having done nothing that anyone will remember."

She opened her eyes and found herself meeting Lucian's gaze. They'd given essentially the same answer—both seeking the crown to validate their existence, to prove their lives mattered.

The first truth is spoken, the Keeper said. *Now the second question. What will you sacrifice to bear the crown's burden?*

"Everything," Lucian said without hesitation. "I've already proven that. I've given up magic, family, normal human connection. I've spent two decades preparing myself, disciplining myself, learning to control the power that once controlled me. I'll sacrifice whatever else is required."

You speak of past sacrifices, the Keeper said. *I ask about future ones. The crown does not reward what you have already lost. It demands what you still hold dear. So I ask again—what will you sacrifice?*

Lucian was silent longer this time. When he spoke, the words were bitter. "My solitude. My isolation. The crown's guardian cannot stand alone— you've made that clear through the trials. I'll have to trust others again. Work with them. Risk caring about them. Risk losing them as I lost my family."

The thought clearly terrified him more than any physical danger could.

And you? The Keeper turned to Brynn. *What will you sacrifice?*

"My certainty," Brynn said after a moment's thought. "The belief that I know the right answer, the right path. Being a guardian means making impossible choices where every option costs something. It means accepting that I'll make mistakes, that people will suffer because of my decisions, and I'll have to live with that forever."

She looked at Thomas and Kira outside the circle—her friends, her anchors.

"It means understanding that I can't protect everyone I care about. That I might have to make choices that hurt them or put them at risk for the greater balance. And I'll have to be strong enough to make those choices anyway, even knowing what it costs."

The second truth is spoken, the Keeper acknowledged. *Now the final question, and the most important. What do you fear most about claiming the crown?*

"That I'll fail," Lucian said without hesitation. "That despite all my preparation, all my study, all my sacrifice, I'll still prove unworthy. That the crown will reject me, or that I'll claim it but still be unable to prevent the disasters I've spent twenty years dreading. That everything I've done, everyone I've lost, will have been for nothing."

And you?

"That I'll succeed," Brynn said quietly.

Lucian's head snapped toward her in shock. Even Thomas and Kira looked surprised.

"Explain," the Keeper commanded.

"If I fail," Brynn said slowly, working through the thought even as she spoke it, "then it's done. The burden passes to someone else. My responsibility ends. But if I succeed—if I claim the crown and become its guardian—then the burden never ends."

She felt tears pricking her eyes but didn't let them fall.

"Every day for the rest of my life, I'll carry that weight. I'll make decisions that affect thousands, maybe millions. I'll have to balance competing goods, choose between terrible options, live with the consequences of choices no one should have to make. Failure would be painful but brief. Success means a lifetime of pain, of doubt, of being responsible for things I can't fully control."

"Then step aside," Lucian said urgently. "You don't want this. You just said so. Let me take that burden. Let me carry what I've been preparing to carry for twenty years."

"No," Brynn said, and her voice was steady now. "Because wanting it or not wanting it isn't what matters. You're right that I'm terrified of success. But I'm more terrified of failing those who believed in me. Of wasting my grandmother's sacrifice. Of letting the balance tip because I was too afraid to accept my calling."

She met the Keeper's featureless face directly.

"I don't want the crown's burden. But I accept it anyway. Not because I'm eager for power or confident I won't fail, but because it's mine to carry whether I want it or not. That's the difference between Lucian and me—he wants to earn worthiness through preparation and discipline. I'm accepting that worthiness isn't something you earn. It's something you're called to, ready or not. And then you do your best to live up to that calling every single day."

The Keeper was silent for a long moment. Its crystalline form pulsed with inner light, and Brynn felt waves of something—emotion? judgment? understanding?—radiating from it.

Then it spoke, its voice resonating with finality:

The challenge is complete. The truth has been spoken by both seekers. And my judgment is rendered.

The Keeper turned fully toward Lucian.

You seek the crown to heal yourself, to make meaning from suffering. This is not wrong, but it is not sufficient. The crown's guardian must serve the balance, not their own need for redemption. You have spent twenty years preparing your mind and power, but you have not prepared your heart. You remain broken, and you seek the crown to make yourself whole. This is the wrong order.

Lucian's face crumpled. "No. No, I've given everything—"

You have given much, the Keeper acknowledged, and its voice was not unkind. *But you have given it to yourself, not to the balance. Your service would be tainted by your need. You would make decisions based not on what serves the balance but on what proves your worthiness. I am sorry, seeker. You are not the one.*

The circle of light around Lucian faded. He stumbled backward, catching himself on his staff, and for a moment Brynn saw naked anguish on his face—twenty years of preparation, of hope, of giving meaning to his suffering, all stripped away in an instant.

Then something else crossed his features. Relief? Grief? Perhaps both.

The Keeper turned to Brynn, and the light around her intensified until she had to squint against its brilliance.

You fear success more than failure. You doubt your worthiness. You acknowledge your inexperience and limitations. These should be weaknesses, yet they are your greatest strengths.

The crystalline figure raised both hands, and Brynn felt power flowing into her—not the crown's power yet, but something else. Recognition. Acceptance. Blessing.

You do not seek the crown to heal yourself or prove your worth. You seek it because you were called, and you accept that calling despite your fears. You understand that the guardian serves the balance, not themselves. You know you will make mistakes, and you will bear that knowledge with humility rather than arrogance.

The Keeper's voice grew stronger, filling not just the circle but the entire valley.

Most importantly, you understand that the guardian does not stand alone. You have proven this through the trials—you trust your companions, you accept their support, you share the burden rather than hoarding it. This is what makes a true guardian. This is what your grandmother knew when she walked away from the crown all those years ago, trusting that the right guardian would come.

The light became almost unbearable, and Brynn felt something settling into place deep in her chest—not physical but profound. A door opening. A path clearing. A destiny accepted.

Brynn Thornwick, granddaughter of Aubre, I name you worthy. The crown awaits in the heart of this valley. Go and claim what is yours.

The circle of light faded. Brynn found herself standing in the valley once more, Thomas and Kira rushing to her side.

"You did it," Thomas said, his voice full of wonder. "The Keeper chose you."

"Not chose," Brynn corrected, still feeling the echo of that vast presence. "Confirmed. The choice was made long ago, before I was born. The Keeper just... verified it."

She looked at Lucian, who stood apart, leaning heavily on his staff. The dark veins had spread further up his neck, nearly reaching his jaw. He met her eyes, and she saw something in his gaze she hadn't expected—not hatred or envy, but understanding. And perhaps, beneath it all, peace.

"I was wrong," he said quietly. "The Keeper was right. I sought the crown for the wrong reasons, and some part of me knew it all along. I just..." He trailed off, then smiled—a real smile, sad but genuine. "Your grandmother saw you in her vision twenty years ago. She knew, even then, that you would be the one. Not me."

"What will you do now?" Kira asked.

Lucian glanced at his splinted leg, at the dark veins crawling across his skin, at the valley around them. "Rest, I suppose. Heal, if I can. Think about what the Keeper said." He met Brynn's eyes again. "The magic I used to get here... it's killing me. Slowly, but killing me nonetheless. I have perhaps a few days left. Maybe a week if I'm lucky."

"We can help you—" Brynn started, but he shook his head.

"No. This is the price I chose to pay. I knew what would happen when I channeled that much power through a body that had forsworn magic for twenty years." He straightened as much as he could. "But I won't die here. Not yet. I have... things to make right before the end."

He looked at all three of them—Brynn, Thomas, Kira—and something in his expression softened.

"The crown is in the valley's heart. You'll know it when you see it. But Brynn—" He paused. "Don't make my mistakes. Don't let the burden consume you. Don't think you have to carry it alone. You have something I never had—people who stand with you not because they have to, but because they choose to. Don't waste that gift."

"I won't," Brynn promised.

Lucian nodded once, then turned and began limping back toward the valley's entrance. Each step looked agonizing, but he didn't ask for help or look back.

They watched him go in silence. When he finally disappeared behind a crystal formation, Kira spoke softly: "Do you think we'll see him again?"

"I don't know," Brynn said honestly. "But I hope so. I hope he finds whatever peace he's looking for."

Thomas put a hand on her shoulder. "The crown is waiting."

Brynn nodded. The pull was there, stronger than ever—not painful but insistent, like a compass needle drawn to true north. She could feel it now, deep in the valley's center, pulsing in rhythm with her own heartbeat.

"Then let's not keep it waiting any longer," she said.

They walked deeper into the Crystal Valley, leaving behind the circle where judgment had been rendered and moving toward the place where everything would change.

The sun was beginning its descent toward the western peaks, painting the crystals in shades of amber and rose and gold. The valley sang around them, harmonics building as they approached the center. And with each step, Brynn felt the weight of destiny pressing down on her shoulders—heavy, yes, but also somehow right.

Her grandmother had walked away from this moment. Had chosen to wait, to prepare the next guardian instead of claiming the power herself.

Brynn wouldn't walk away. Couldn't walk away, even if she wanted to.

The crown was calling.

And she was finally ready to answer.

Chapter 11: Claiming The Crown

The valley's heart revealed itself gradually, like a secret being unwrapped with reverent hands.

As Brynn, Thomas, and Kira walked deeper into the Crystal Valley, the formations around them grew larger, more elaborate. What had been simple spires and columns at the valley's edge became towering sculptures that defied logic—crystals that spiraled upward in impossible helixes, structures that bent light into colors that had no names, formations that seemed to shift and change when viewed from different angles.

The singing grew louder too. Each crystal hummed with its own frequency, and together they created a symphony that Brynn felt as much as heard. The music resonated in her bones, in her blood, in the very rhythm of her heartbeat. It was beautiful and overwhelming and ancient beyond comprehension.

"It's like walking through a cathedral made of frozen light," Kira whispered, her voice hushed with awe.

Thomas said nothing, but his hand rested on his sword hilt—not from fear, Brynn thought, but from habit. He was her anchor, her protector, even here in this place where physical protection seemed almost irrelevant compared to the weight of magic pressing down on them.

The map in Brynn's jacket had gone silent. No longer pulsing, no longer warm. Its work was done. It had brought her here, to this moment, and now it waited—just parchment and ink again—for whatever came next.

But the pull was stronger than ever. Brynn could feel the crown now with a clarity that bordered on painful. It was close. So close. Just ahead, beyond this next formation, past that crystalline arch...

They rounded a final curve, and the valley opened before them into a circular depression perhaps a hundred feet across. The ground sloped gently downward toward the center, and the crystals here were different—smaller, more delicate, growing in intricate patterns that looked almost deliberate. Like a garden. Like an offering.

And in the exact center, on a pedestal of crystal that seemed to grow organically from the earth itself, rested the Crimson Crown.

Brynn's breath caught.

It was smaller than she'd imagined—delicate, almost fragile-looking, made of metal that gleamed deep red like rubies given form. The crown's band was intricately worked with symbols that matched those on her map, flowing and shifting as if the metal itself was alive. Set into it at regular intervals were actual gemstones that pulsed with their own inner light—not bright, but steady, like heartbeats made visible.

It wasn't the ostentatious crown of a king or emperor, all gold and size and declaration of power. It was something subtler, more profound. Power condensed into art. Purpose made manifest. A promise forged in starfire and bound with oaths older than language.

"It's beautiful," Brynn whispered.

"It's been waiting," Kira said softly, and Brynn realized she was right. There was no dust on the crown, no weathering or tarnish despite the years— decades, centuries—it must have rested here. The

Keeper had maintained it. Protected it. Preserved it for this moment.

For her.

"Are you ready?" Thomas asked quietly, moving to stand beside her.

Brynn wanted to say yes. Wanted to be confident, certain, ready. But honesty won out.

"No," she admitted. "I'm terrified. Everything I told the Keeper was true—I'm afraid of what happens after I claim it. Afraid of failing. Afraid of succeeding. Afraid of becoming something that can't protect the people I love."

Thomas took her hand, his grip warm and solid and real. "Then be afraid. But do it anyway."

Kira moved to her other side, not touching but present. Steady. "You don't have to be fearless to be brave. You just have to keep moving forward despite the fear."

Brynn looked at them both—her companions, her friends, her anchors in this impossible moment. Then she looked at the crown, pulsing gently on its pedestal, waiting with the patience of ages.

"Together," she said. "Whatever comes next, we face it together."

"Always," Thomas replied.

"Always," Kira echoed.

Brynn took a deep breath and began descending into the depression.

Immediately, she felt resistance—not physical but magical. The air itself seemed to thicken, to push back against her, testing her determination. Each step required effort, like walking through water that grew denser with every pace. The crown's power surrounded her, evaluating, measuring, deciding if she was truly worthy or if the Keeper's judgment had been wrong.

Behind her, she heard Thomas take a step forward.

"No," Brynn said, not turning around. "This part I have to do alone."

She felt rather than saw his reluctant acceptance. Felt Kira's hand on his arm, holding him back.

Brynn forced herself forward, and as she did, visions began to flash before her eyes—not the personal visions of the altar but something grander, more impersonal. History made visible. Memory made manifest.

She saw the crown's creation.

The Celestial Smiths stood in a forge that existed between dimensions, in a space that was neither fully real nor fully imagined. They were tall —impossibly tall—and luminous, their forms constantly shifting as if they couldn't quite settle on a single shape. Their hands moved with impossible precision, shaping reality itself with hammer and will.

The crown took form slowly, carefully, with painstaking attention to every detail. This wasn't just metalwork. This was the weaving of purpose into matter, the binding of intention into form. Each symbol carved into the band held meaning. Each gemstone was chosen not for beauty but for the specific frequency it would resonate at, the particular aspect of balance it would help maintain.

Balance, the Smiths sang as they worked, their voices creating harmonics that made the forge itself vibrate. *Light and shadow. Order and chaos.*

Creation and destruction. All must be held in tension, in equilibrium, or reality itself unravels.

The vision shifted.

She saw the first guardian—a woman whose name had been lost to time—claiming the crown with trembling hands. Saw the moment it settled onto her brow and the surge of knowledge, of responsibility, of terrible beautiful power that flooded through her. Saw her expression shift from wonder to understanding to grim determination.

Saw her first decision as guardian—choosing to let a city fall to darkness rather than upset the balance by flooding it with too much light. Saw the weight of that choice in her eyes. Saw her weep for the lives lost while knowing she'd made the right decision.

The balance requires sacrifice, her voice echoed across centuries. *Requires choices that have no good answers. Only necessary ones.*

The visions accelerated.

Centuries of guardians flashed past like pages in a book being rapidly thumbed through. Each one different. Each one facing their own era's challenges. Wars and plagues and natural disasters and threats from beyond the veil of reality. Each guardian making impossible choices, bearing impossible burdens, protecting a balance that most people didn't even know existed.

And each one, eventually, passing the crown to the next. Some died in battle. Some grew old and weary and chose their successor before death claimed them. But all of them, in the end, let go. Released the burden to the next guardian and found whatever peace they could in knowing they'd done their part.

Then came Lyra Stormblade.

Brynn saw her clearly—fierce and brilliant, with eyes like steel and a smile that could cut glass. She was the last guardian, the one who'd fought in the Shadow Wars, the one who'd held the line when reality itself was tearing apart.

The visions showed those final battles. Showed Lyra wielding the crown's power with skill born of decades of practice, pushing back forces that should have been unstoppable. But there were too many breaches, too many fronts, too much darkness pouring through.

In the end, cornered and dying, she'd made a choice.

Rather than let the Shadow Court claim the crown—rather than let it fall into hands that would corrupt its purpose—she'd hidden it. Used the last of her strength to create the map, to bind it with magic that would only reveal itself to the next worthy guardian. And then, with her final breath, she'd sealed the Shadow Court away, created a prison that would hold them.

For a time.

Not forever, Lyra's voice whispered across the years. *I bought time, not victory. The prison weakens with every passing year. Eventually, it will fail. Unless...*

Unless someone claimed the crown. Learned its power. Finished what Lyra had started.

The vision shifted again, and Brynn saw her grandmother.

Young, fierce, beautiful Aubre standing at the ancient altar in the Misty Mountains. The map had called her. She had journeyed alone, been tested by the altar's trial, and been named worthy. The path to the Crystal Valley lay open before her. The crown waited.

Aubre stood at the altar's center, catching her breath after the trial, and the ancient stones granted her a vision—a gift given to those deemed truly worthy. A glimpse of what might come.

In that vision, Aubre saw a girl. Her granddaughter—not yet born, not even conceived, but real nonetheless. She saw Brynn standing at this very altar years in the future, passing the same trial. Saw her continuing where Aubre might have stopped. Saw her ready in ways that Aubre wasn't, strong in ways that Aubre couldn't be.

And in that moment, Aubre understood.

The crown wasn't calling her to claim it. The crown was calling her to prepare the one who would.

Aubre opened her eyes, the vision fading. She looked toward the north, where the Crystal Valley waited with its precious burden. She could go there. Could claim the crown. Could become the guardian her generation needed.

But she wouldn't be the guardian the next generation needed. That role belonged to someone else. Someone not yet born.

Aubre made her choice.

She turned away from the path to the Crystal Valley. Descended from the altar without looking back. And she walked away from destiny—not in cowardice, but in wisdom. Understanding that sometimes the greatest act of heroism is stepping aside for someone better suited to the task.

She never touched the crown. Never even saw it. Never met the Keeper face to face.

But she did send a message. Through magic, through will, through the same connection that had shown her the vision. She sent her understanding to the Keeper, to the crown itself, asking them to wait.

Wait for her, Aubre's voice echoed across the years, carried on winds of magic to the guardian who watched over the crown. *Wait for my granddaughter. She'll come when the time is right. And when she does, she'll be ready for what I never could be.*

The Keeper had listened. Had waited. Had maintained the crown through twenty additional years, trusting that Aubre's vision was true.

And now Brynn stood where her grandmother never had, reaching for what her grandmother had refused.

The visions released Brynn abruptly.

She found herself standing directly before the pedestal, her hand extended, fingers inches from the crown. She hadn't consciously walked the final steps. Her body had moved while her mind was lost in history.

The crown waited.

Brynn took one final breath, steadying herself, then reached out and touched it.

The world exploded into sensation.

Knowledge flooded into her mind—not drowning her but filling her, becoming part of her. She understood suddenly and completely how everything connected. Saw the web of cause and effect that held reality together. Felt the places where light grew too strong and needed tempering, where shadow grew too deep and needed illumination. Understood the delicate dance of balance that the crown existed to maintain.

And she saw the Shadow Court.

Not as abstract concept but as reality. They were real, they were vast, and they were imprisoned—locked away in a dimension that bordered reality but couldn't quite touch it. The barriers that held them were weakening, cracks spreading through the cosmic prison that Lyra Stormblade had created with her dying breath.

The cracks had grown larger in the twenty years since her grandmother had walked away. Twenty years without an active guardian. Twenty years of the prison slowly failing, the boundaries between dimensions growing thin.

The Shadow Court sensed her touch on the crown. She felt their attention turn toward her like the eye of a malevolent god, and she heard their voice—cold, ancient, hungry.

So, they whispered across dimensions. *A new guardian rises. How... unfortunate for you.*

Their presence was overwhelming—not just one consciousness but many, all merged together into something greater and more terrible than the sum of its parts. They pressed against the barriers of their prison, testing, probing, searching for weaknesses.

And they were finding them.

Brynn saw the breaches clearly now—tears in reality where the prison had worn thin, where shadow was beginning to leak through into the world. Three major breaches, dozens of minor ones. And at the largest breach, something was gathering. Something vast and powerful, preparing to push through the moment the barrier failed completely.

Do you accept? A different voice asked—the crown itself, or perhaps the collective wisdom of all the guardians who'd come before. *Do you accept this burden, knowing what you face? The Shadow Court rises. They must be stopped, sealed away permanently. This is the guardian's purpose. This is the guardian's war.*

"I accept," Brynn said, her voice steady despite the terror coursing through her. "I accept the burden. I accept the responsibility. I'll stop them."

Then you may borrow my power, the crown said, and Brynn felt something shift. *But you have *not yet earned the right to claim me fully. You have proven your heart through the trials. You have been named worthy by the Keeper. But a guardian is not made through trials alone. A guardian is forged through deeds.*

Brynn felt the crown's presence in her mind pull back slightly even as power continued to flow into her.

Use my power, the crown instructed. *Learn to wield it. Fight the forces that threaten the balance. Seal the Shadow Court back into their prison, repair what has been broken. Only when you have completed this task—only when you have proven yourself not just worthy but capable—will I be fully yours to claim.*

"How long do I have?" Brynn asked.

As long as it takes, the crown replied. *But know this—every day you delay, the barriers weaken further. The Shadow Court sends their servants through the cracks. Shadow beasts, corrupted creatures, beings of pure chaos. They will hunt you. They will test you. They will try to break you before you can seal them away forever.*

"Then I'll start now," Brynn said.

Good. But first, take me with you. Wear me, though I am not yet yours. Let the world see that a guardian walks among them once more. Let the Shadow Court know their prison will be reinforced. Let hope return to those who have lived without it.

Brynn lifted the crown from its pedestal with shaking hands. The moment her fingers closed around it, she felt it warm against her skin—welcoming but not quite accepting, like a tool she was permitted to use but not yet to own.

The metal was heavier than it looked, but the weight felt right somehow. Purposeful. As if it had substance beyond the merely physical.

She raised it slowly, reverently, and settled it onto her head.

It fit perfectly.

The crown was warm against her brow, not uncomfortably but distinctly present. Power flowed through her immediately—controlled, channeled, purposeful. She could feel the balance it represented, could sense the places where adjustment was needed, where her intervention would be required.

And she could feel the Shadow Court, watching, waiting, preparing to test her.

Brynn opened her eyes and found Thomas and Kira staring at her with expressions of awe.

"You're glowing," Thomas said softly. "Like you're made of light."

Brynn looked down at her hands and saw it was true. A soft radiance emanated from her skin, not bright enough to hurt but distinctly visible. The crown's power, made manifest.

"The crown has accepted me," Brynn said, though even as she spoke the words she knew they weren't quite accurate. "But not completely. Not yet."

"What do you mean?" Kira asked.

"I mean I have to earn it," Brynn explained, touching the crown gently. She could feel it responding to her thoughts, her intentions, ready to channel power when she needed it but still maintaining a slight distance. Still evaluating. "The trials proved my heart. But now I have to prove my strength. The Shadow Court is rising—they've been imprisoned since the Shadow Wars, but the barriers are failing. I have to seal them back, permanently. Only then will the crown truly be mine."

She climbed back up from the depression, and with each step she felt more solid, more real, more present than she'd ever felt in her life. The crown wasn't just resting on her head—it was becoming part of her, teaching her, preparing her for what came next.

Thomas and Kira met her at the top of the depression.

"How do we seal them?" Thomas asked.

"I don't know yet," Brynn admitted. "The crown will teach me as we go. But it told me they're already sending servants through the cracks—shadow beasts, corrupted creatures. We'll encounter them. Soon."

"Then we'd better be ready," Kira said, checking her knife.

Brynn touched the crown again, feeling its power respond instantly to her thought. She wasn't just borrowing it—she was learning to use it, to channel it, to make it an extension of her will. But it was clear that full mastery, full ownership, would only come after she'd proven herself in battle.

"The Shadow Court knows I'm here now," Brynn said quietly, feeling their attention like weight pressing against her mind. "They felt me touch the crown. They're watching. Waiting."

"Let them watch," Thomas said, his hand on his sword. "We'll be ready."

As if in response to his words, the temperature dropped.

Not gradually but all at once, like someone had thrown open a door to winter. Their breath misted in the suddenly frigid air, and frost began forming on the crystals around them—something that should have been impossible given the valley's warmth moments before.

"Brynn," Kira said, her voice tight with fear. "What's happening?"

Brynn reached out with the crown's awareness —an instinct she hadn't known she possessed—and felt it. A tear in reality, a crack in the barriers between dimensions. Close. Very close. Perhaps at the valley's edge.

The Shadow Court was pushing through.

"They're here," Brynn said, her voice steadier than she felt. "They're not waiting. They're testing me now. The first battle is beginning."

From the edges of the valley, shadows began to flow. Not natural shadows cast by objects blocking light, but darkness given form and purpose. They coalesced into shapes Brynn recognized from the altar's battle—shadow beasts, but larger now, more solid, more dangerous.

Dozens of them.

They moved with predatory grace, flowing between the crystal formations like liquid darkness. Their eyes glowed red in the gathering gloom, and their growls resonated with frequencies that made Brynn's bones ache.

"There are too many," Kira whispered.

"Then we make ourselves harder to kill," Thomas said, drawing his sword. The blade caught the fading sunlight and held it, gleaming.

Brynn reached for the crown's power, and it responded instantly. Knowledge flooded into her—not just how to wield the power, but what it cost, what it demanded, how to balance strength with wisdom. The crown wouldn't let her simply unleash destruction. Every use of power required intention, purpose, understanding of consequences.

"Stay close to me," Brynn commanded, and raised both hands.

Light burst forth—pure white radiance that pushed back the shadows, creating a bubble of protection around the three of them. The shadow beasts recoiled but didn't retreat. They circled, testing the barrier, searching for weaknesses.

Brynn felt the drain immediately. Holding this much power, this much light, required constant effort. She could maintain it, but not forever. Eventually, she'd exhaust herself.

"We can't just stand here," Thomas said, echoing her thoughts.

"No," Brynn agreed. "We fight our way out. Together."

She let the barrier drop and instead channeled the crown's power into focused strikes—beams of light that lanced through shadow beasts, destroying them where they stood. Each strike felt right, precise, like the crown was guiding her hand while letting her make the final choices.

Thomas and Kira fought at her sides, protecting her flanks while she wielded the crown's power. Thomas's sword cut through shadow flesh that should have been intangible but wasn't—the blade seeming to sense where the beasts were most vulnerable. Kira moved with surprising grace, her knife finding throats and hearts with deadly accuracy.

They fought their way across the valley floor, step by step, destroying shadow beasts that kept coming. For every one they killed, two more seemed to emerge from the darkness gathering at the valley's edges.

"There's no end to them!" Kira shouted over the sounds of battle.

"The breach is still open," Brynn said, destroying three beasts with a single sweeping burst of light. "They'll keep coming until I seal it."

"Then seal it!" Thomas said, his sword cutting through another beast.

"I don't know how!" Brynn admitted. The crown held the knowledge, but it was locked away, not yet accessible. She needed to prove herself first, needed to earn the right to access the deeper powers.

A massive shadow beast—larger than any they'd faced—burst through the circle of smaller creatures. It was bear-like but wrong, with too many limbs and a mouth that opened far wider than any natural animal's could. It lunged directly at Brynn.

Thomas intercepted it, his sword meeting claws that should have shattered steel but didn't. The impact sent him stumbling backward, but he held the line.

Brynn gathered power, feeling the crown respond to her desperate need. She thrust both hands forward and released everything she had—not a focused beam but an explosion of pure light that consumed the massive beast entirely.

It shrieked—a sound like reality tearing—and dissolved into nothing.

The smaller beasts hesitated, suddenly uncertain. Their alpha had fallen. Their prey had teeth.

"Now!" Brynn shouted. "While they're confused!"

They ran.

Not in panic, but strategically, fighting their way toward the valley's entrance while the shadow beasts regrouped. Brynn's power carved a path through the darkness. Thomas and Kira protected her from attacks she didn't see coming.

They were perhaps fifty feet from the valley's edge when Brynn felt it—a presence that made the shadow beasts seem like mere insects in comparison. Something vast was pushing through the breach. Something that the crown recognized with terror.

A lieutenant, the crown's voice whispered in her mind. *One of the Shadow Court's generals. You're not ready to face this. Not yet. RUN.*

"RUN!" Brynn shouted to her companions, echoing the crown's command.

They didn't question her. They ran.

Behind them, something emerged from the shadows—a figure that stood twelve feet tall, humanoid but wrong in ways that hurt to look at directly. Its presence warped reality around it, bending light and sound and sense into impossible configurations.

It spoke, and its voice was like broken glass scraping against bone:

"Little guardian. New and untested. You cannot seal us. You will fail. And when you do, we will remake your world in our image."

Brynn didn't look back. She channeled power into her legs, into her companions, lending them speed beyond natural limits. They burst from the Crystal Valley into the mountain passage beyond, and Brynn felt the moment they crossed some invisible boundary.

The Shadow Court lieutenant didn't follow.

Couldn't follow, not yet. Whatever barrier the Keeper maintained around the valley still held, still prevented the worst from emerging.

But that barrier wouldn't hold forever.

Brynn, Thomas, and Kira collapsed against the passage wall, gasping for breath. The crown on Brynn's head still glowed softly, still pulsed with power, but she could feel her own exhaustion like a weight settling into her bones.

"What was that?" Kira asked when she could speak.

"A lieutenant of the Shadow Court," Brynn said. "One of their generals. The crown says there are three of them. Each one controls a major breach point. Each one must be defeated before I can seal the Shadow Court away permanently."

"And we just ran from the first one," Thomas said.

"Because we weren't ready," Brynn replied. "Because I'm not ready. Not yet." She touched the crown. "I need to learn. To practice. To understand what this power can really do."

She looked at her friends—exhausted, frightened, but still standing. Still with her.

"The Shadow Court said we'd fail," Brynn said quietly. "They're wrong. We won't fail. But we also can't rush this. We need to be smart. Strategic. We need to find the other breaches, learn what we're facing, and then—when we're ready—we seal them all."

"Where do we start?" Kira asked.

Brynn closed her eyes, reaching out with the crown's awareness. She could feel the breaches now—three major ones, scattered across the land. The closest was... northwest. Perhaps five days' journey. In a place the crown called the Corrupted Forest.

"Northwest," Brynn said, opening her eyes. "Five days from here. There's another breach. We go there next."

"And if we're not strong enough when we get there?" Thomas asked.

"Then we retreat again," Brynn said. "We keep retreating until we are strong enough. Because the alternative—failing, letting the Shadow Court break free—that's not an option."

She stood, still exhausted but determined.

"The first battle is over. We survived. We learned. And now we keep moving forward."

The crown pulsed against her brow, and Brynn felt its approval. This was how guardians were forged—not through single moments of glory but through persistence, through learning, through refusing to give up even when the odds seemed impossible.

They had a long road ahead.

But they would walk it together.

And somehow, some way, they would find a way to seal the Shadow Court back into their prison before it was too late.

Chapter 12: The First Battle

The mountain passage felt different after what they'd seen.

The same stone walls, the same narrow path winding between peaks—but everything had changed. Brynn could feel the crown's weight on her head, not heavy but present, a constant reminder of what she'd claimed and what still lay ahead. And beneath that weight, exhaustion settled into her bones like lead.

"We need to rest," Thomas said, catching Brynn's arm as she stumbled over loose rock. "You're dead on your feet."

"We're too close," Brynn protested, though she knew he was right. Her legs felt like water, and the crown's glow had dimmed to barely visible. "That lieutenant—"

"Can't follow us here," Kira finished. "The Keeper's barrier holds. Thomas is right. We rest now or we collapse later at a worse time."

Brynn wanted to argue, but her body made the decision for her. Her knees buckled, and only Thomas's quick reflexes kept her from hitting the ground.

"That settles it," he said, lowering her gently to sit against the passage wall. "We camp here."

"Here" was a widening in the passage where fallen rocks created a natural shelter of sorts. Not ideal, but defensible. Thomas immediately began checking the perimeter while Kira pulled food and water from their packs.

Brynn closed her eyes, reaching inward to assess the damage. Using the crown's power had cost more than she'd realized. It wasn't just physical exhaustion—something deeper had been drained. Her spirit, maybe. Her life force. Whatever allowed her to channel the crown's magic.

You pushed too hard, the crown's voice murmured in her mind, gentler now than before. *The power I give is not unlimited. It flows through you, and you are still learning how much you can safely channel.*

"How do I learn?" Brynn whispered aloud.

Practice. Rest. Growth. A guardian is not made in a day, young one. Lyra Stormblade trained for years before she faced her first true battle.

"We don't have years," Brynn said.

Then you will learn faster. But you must also learn smarter. Power without wisdom destroys the wielder as surely as it destroys her enemies.

Brynn opened her eyes to find Thomas crouching before her, offering a water skin. She drank gratefully, the cold water clearing some of the fog from her mind.

"What did you just say?" Thomas asked. "About not having years?"

"The crown says I need more training," Brynn explained. "That Lyra Stormblade trained for years before facing real battles. But the breaches are opening now. The Shadow Court is pushing through now."

"Then we adapt," Kira said, settling beside them with dried meat and bread. "We train while we travel. Practice while we rest. Learn on the move."

Thomas nodded. "What do you need? What can we do to help?"

The question made Brynn's throat tight. They didn't have to help. They could leave, go back to Thornhaven, live normal lives. But they stayed. Chose to stay.

"I need to understand the crown's limits," Brynn said. "And my own. I need to know how much power I can channel safely, how long I can maintain it, how fast I can recover."

"So we test it," Thomas said. "Controlled practice. Small uses of power, increasing gradually."

"And we need to know what we're really facing," Kira added. "Those shadow beasts—are they the worst of it? Or just the beginning?"

Brynn touched the crown, feeling it respond to her question. Knowledge flowed into her mind—not overwhelming this time, just what she needed to know.

"The shadow beasts are the weakest servants," she said slowly, processing what the crown was showing her. "Above them are shadow warriors—humanoid, intelligent, harder to kill. Above those are corrupted creatures—things from our world that the Shadow Court has twisted into weapons."

"Like what?" Thomas asked.

"Animals. People. Anything with enough life force to corrupt." Brynn shuddered at the images the crown was showing her. "And then there are the three lieutenants. Each one commands an army. Each one guards a major breach."

"What about the Shadow Court itself?" Kira asked. "The actual... whatever they are. Can they come through?"

"Not yet," Brynn said. "Not unless all three breaches fully open. Right now, they're still mostly sealed. But every day the barriers weaken.

Eventually—maybe weeks, maybe months—they'll break through completely unless I seal them."

Thomas pulled out a piece of charcoal and began sketching on a flat rock. "So we have three targets. Three lieutenants, three breaches. What's the order? Which one first?"

Brynn reached out with the crown's awareness, feeling for the breaches. "The closest is northwest. The Corrupted Forest. That lieutenant commands the shadow beasts and corrupted animals. It's the weakest of the three."

"Weakest meaning easiest to defeat?" Kira asked hopefully.

"Weakest meaning it will only probably kill us instead of definitely kill us," Brynn said dryly. "But yes, if we're going to learn by doing, that's where we start."

Thomas studied his rough map. "Five days northwest. What's after that?"

"The second breach is near Thornhaven," Brynn said quietly. "Maybe two days' journey from home. That lieutenant commands shadow warriors and corrupted people. It's stronger."

Thomas's face went pale. "Our home is that close to a breach?"

"It's been growing for years," Brynn said. "Slowly. The villagers probably don't even know—they just think the forest nearby is dangerous, that strange things happen after dark. But yes. That's the second target."

"And the third?" Kira prompted.

"The Shadow Peaks," Brynn said, remembering what the crown had shown her. "Beyond the Fang Mountains, in a place where reality is already thin. That's where the Shadow King waits—the leader of the three lieutenants. That breach is the largest, the most dangerous. If I don't seal the other two first, I'll have no chance against him."

They sat in silence, absorbing the scale of what lay ahead. Three battles. Three breaches. And they had to win all three or everything would be lost.

"Then we rest tonight," Thomas said finally, his voice firm with decision. "Tomorrow we start training. And then we head northwest."

"We should reach the Corrupted Forest in five days if we push," Kira calculated. "That gives you five days to practice, to learn your limits."

"Five days to become strong enough to face a lieutenant of the Shadow Court," Brynn said. It sounded impossible even as she said it.

"You won't be alone," Thomas reminded her. "We fight together. That's how we've survived everything so far."

"Speaking of which," Kira said, pulling her knife and examining the blade. "I need a better weapon. This knife is fine for throats and cooking, but shadow beasts need more reach."

"We passed a town two days back," Thomas said. "Small place, but it had a blacksmith. We could stop there tomorrow, get you equipped properly. Get all of us better gear."

Brynn nodded, though the idea of stopping felt wrong when time was so short. But Thomas was right—going into battle unprepared was suicide.

"We'll stop at the town," she agreed. "One day to resupply and rest properly. Then we continue to the Corrupted Forest."

They ate in silence, each lost in their own thoughts. The sun had fully set now, darkness filling the passage except for the soft glow from Brynn's crown. It cast strange shadows on the rock walls, making everything look otherworldly.

"I'll take first watch," Thomas volunteered, standing and moving to the passage entrance. "You two sleep. You've earned it."

Kira settled into her bedroll without argument, exhaustion claiming her almost immediately. But Brynn found sleep elusive despite her exhaustion. Every time she closed her eyes, she saw the Shadow Court lieutenant—that impossible figure warping reality around it, promising failure and doom.

You doubt yourself, the crown observed quietly.

"Wouldn't you?" Brynn thought back, not bothering to speak aloud.

Of course. Doubt keeps you cautious. Keeps you questioning your choices. It's when you stop doubting that you become dangerous—not to your enemies, but to everything you're trying to protect.

"Lucian was certain," Brynn said. "Twenty years of preparation, and he was absolutely sure he was ready. You rejected him."

Because his certainty came from need, not wisdom. He needed to be worthy to give his suffering meaning. You doubt because you understand the weight of what you carry. That understanding is worth more than all his preparation.

Brynn touched the crown gently. "Will I be strong enough? When we face that first lieutenant, will I be able to defeat it?"

I don't know, the crown admitted, and the honesty was somehow comforting. *You might. You might not. But you'll be there, trying, fighting with everything you have. And sometimes that's all any guardian can do.*

Brynn finally drifted into uneasy sleep, dreams filled with shadows and light and battles yet to come.

She woke to Thomas shaking her shoulder gently. "Your watch," he murmured. "Nothing's tried to kill us yet. Good sign."

Brynn took her position at the passage entrance, sword across her knees—a weapon she barely knew how to use but carried anyway for the comfort of steel. The crown glowed softly, providing just enough light to see by.

The mountains were silent. No wind, no animals, nothing. Just stone and stars and the weight of destiny pressing down.

Brynn spent her watch practicing what the crown had taught her. Small things—calling light to her palm, dismissing it, calling it again. Shaping it into different forms. Maintaining it for longer periods. Each exercise showed her more about the crown's power and her own limits.

By the time dawn lightened the eastern sky, she could hold a steady sphere of light for nearly an hour before exhaustion forced her to stop. Not much, but better than before.

Thomas and Kira woke to the smell of cooking—Brynn had used a small flame of crown-fire to heat water for a thin porridge made from their dwindling supplies.

"We definitely need to resupply," Kira said, eyeing the meager breakfast.

They ate quickly and set off down the mountain, leaving the Crystal Valley and the Keeper behind. The path was easier going down than up, and they made good time despite their exhaustion.

Around midday, they emerged from the mountains into rolling foothills covered in pine forest. The town Thomas had mentioned was visible in the distance—a small collection of buildings clustered around a crossroads, smoke rising from chimneys.

"Millbrook," Thomas said, reading a weathered sign at the fork in the road. "Population forty-seven. Or it was last time I passed through."

"You've been here before?" Kira asked.

"Three years ago, delivering tools my father made. Good people. Practical. They won't ask too many questions if we don't volunteer too much information."

"What about the crown?" Brynn asked, touching it self-consciously. "People will notice."

"Cover it," Thomas suggested. "Hood, scarf, something. Say you're recovering from an illness and the light hurts your eyes."

Brynn pulled her hood up, arranging it to shadow her face and hide the crown's glow. It wasn't perfect, but it would have to do.

They entered Millbrook cautiously, but the town seemed normal enough. People going about their business, merchants hawking wares, children playing in the street. No shadow beasts, no signs of corruption.

The blacksmith's forge was exactly where Thomas remembered—a sturdy building on the town's edge, smoke pouring from its chimney and the ring of hammer on anvil echoing across the square.

A broad-shouldered man looked up as they approached, his face weathered and kind. "Help you folks?"

"We need weapons," Thomas said. "And maybe armor if you have any ready-made."

The blacksmith's eyes sharpened, assessing them. "Running toward trouble or away from it?"

"Toward," Brynn said honestly.

The man nodded slowly. "Thought so. You've got that look about you. Come inside. Let's see what we can do."

The forge was hot and filled with the smell of coal and metal. Weapons hung on the walls—swords, axes, spears, all well-made if simple.

"For the young lady," the blacksmith said, pulling down a short sword with a wide blade. "Good balance, reaches farther than a knife but not so long you'll tangle yourself in close quarters."

Kira took it, testing the weight. A smile crossed her face. "This will do."

"And for you, miss?" The blacksmith looked at Brynn, then at Thomas. "She already armed?"

"She is," Thomas said carefully. "But she could use—"

"Armor," the blacksmith finished. "Light stuff, won't slow her down. I've got a leather vest with steel plates sewn in. Made it for a merchant's daughter who never came to collect it. Should fit."

He pulled the armor from a chest—supple leather reinforced with small steel plates over vital areas. Well-crafted, flexible, and much better protection than Brynn currently had. "I'll take it," Brynn said. "What's the cost?"

The blacksmith named a price that was fair but would take most of their remaining coin. Brynn paid without hesitation. Their lives were worth more than money.

As Brynn tried on the armor—it fit almost perfectly—the blacksmith moved closer, his voice dropping.

"You're hunting something," he said quietly. "Something dark. I can see it in your eyes."

Brynn met his gaze. "What if I am?"

"Then be careful. There are stories coming from the northwest. Travelers talk about a forest that's gone wrong. Animals acting strange. People who go in but don't come out." He paused. "That's where you're headed, isn't it?"

"Yes," Brynn said simply.

The blacksmith reached behind his counter and pulled out a small pouch. "Take this. Mixture of salt and iron filings. Old folk remedy against dark things. Probably won't help much against what you're facing, but it's what I can offer."

"Thank you," Brynn said, genuinely touched.

"Thank me by coming back alive," the blacksmith replied. "And by stopping whatever's making those forests wrong."

They left the forge properly equipped—Kira with her new sword, Brynn with armor that would actually protect her, Thomas with fresh supplies and information about the road northwest.

They spent the night at Millbrook's small inn, paying for real beds and hot food. Brynn used the time to practice more with the crown, carefully, in the privacy of their room. Small exercises. Building stamina. Learning control.

By morning, she could maintain a shield of light for ninety minutes. Still not enough to fight a lieutenant, but better.

They set off at dawn, heading northwest on a road that quickly narrowed to a trail, then to barely a path. The forest thickened around them, and Brynn felt it—a wrongness in the air, a taste like copper on her tongue.

The corruption was spreading from the breach.

They were getting close.

"Three more days," Thomas estimated, studying the path ahead. "Maybe two if we push hard."

"We push hard," Brynn said. "Every day we delay, the breach grows stronger."

They did push hard, covering ground that should have taken four days in just over two. But the cost showed in their exhaustion, their dwindling supplies, the strain visible in every movement.

The forest changed as they traveled. Trees grew twisted, their bark blackened as if by fire that had never burned. Animals watched them from the shadows—deer with too many eyes, birds with feathers like knives. None attacked, but the threat was constant.

On the third night, they made camp in a clearing that felt less corrupted than the surrounding forest. Brynn could feel why—there was a stone here, ancient and weathered, carved with symbols that matched those on her crown.

"A marker," she said, touching it. "Left by guardians who came before. This place is warded, protected."

"Will it hold?" Kira asked nervously, eyeing the shadows beyond their firelight.

"For tonight," Brynn said. "But we're close now. Very close. Tomorrow we'll reach the breach."

"And the lieutenant?" Thomas asked.

"And the lieutenant," Brynn confirmed.

They sat around the fire, preparing themselves mentally for what came next. Brynn practiced one more time, calling light and shaping it, feeling the crown's power flow through her more smoothly than before. Not perfect, but better.

She could do this. She had to do this.

The night passed without incident, the warded stone keeping the corrupted forest at bay. But when dawn broke, Brynn felt it immediately—a pressure against her mind, a presence probing at the edges of her awareness.

The lieutenant knew they were coming.

And it was waiting.

They broke camp quickly, checking weapons and armor one final time. Brynn adjusted the crown, feeling it pulse with readiness. The power was there, waiting to be channeled. She just had to be strong enough to wield it.

"Stay together," she reminded them. "No matter what happens, we don't separate."

"Together," Thomas agreed.

"Always," Kira added.

They walked into the forest, toward the breach, toward the battle that would prove whether Brynn was truly ready to be a guardian.

The trees grew more twisted the deeper they went. The air grew colder despite the summer sun. And ahead, through the corrupted forest, Brynn could see it—a tear in reality itself, darkness bleeding through into the world.

And standing before the breach, waiting with predatory patience, was the lieutenant.

It was massive—twelve feet of corrupted flesh and shadow, shaped roughly like a stag but wrong in every detail. Too many antlers, branching in impossible directions. Eyes that glowed like coals scattered across its body. A mouth that opened vertically instead of horizontally, lined with teeth like broken glass.

The Lieutenant of the Corrupted Forest.

It spoke, and its voice was the sound of trees screaming as they burned:

"So. The infant guardian comes to play. Come, little light. Let me show you what happens to those who challenge the Shadow Court."

Brynn drew her sword, channeled power through the crown, and stepped forward.

The first battle had truly begun.

Chapter 13: The Corrupted Forest

The lieutenant moved first.

It was faster than anything that size should be—one moment standing still, the next charging across the clearing with speed that blurred reality around it. Brynn barely had time to raise her hands, channeling the crown's power into a shield of light.

The lieutenant hit the barrier like a battering ram.

The impact drove Brynn backward, her boots digging trenches in the earth as she fought to hold the shield. Power drained from her at an alarming rate—this creature was far stronger than the shadow beasts had been.

Thomas and Kira attacked from the sides, trying to draw the lieutenant's attention. Thomas's sword struck its flank, and to Brynn's shock, the blade bit deep. Dark ichor flowed from the wound, steaming where it hit the ground.

The lieutenant whirled, faster than thought, one massive antler sweeping toward Thomas. He ducked under it, barely, the tines passing close enough to tear his shirt.

Kira darted in, her new sword striking at the creature's legs. She hit something vital—the lieutenant stumbled, crying out in pain and rage.

"It can be hurt!" Kira shouted. "It's not invulnerable!"

Brynn dropped the shield and channeled power into an attack instead—a beam of concentrated light aimed at the lieutenant's center mass. The crown guided her aim, and the beam struck true, burning into corrupted flesh.

The lieutenant shrieked, a sound that made the corrupted trees around them wither further. It staggered but didn't fall.

"Persistent little lights," it hissed. "But persistence without power is just slow death."

It raised one massive hoof and slammed it into the ground. The earth erupted, shadow-thorns bursting from the soil like spears. Brynn dove aside, felt one graze her arm despite the armor. The touch burned like ice and fire combined.

Thomas wasn't as lucky. A thorn caught his leg, piercing through cloth and skin. He cried out but didn't fall, instead gritting his teeth and cutting the thorn away with his sword.

"Thomas!" Brynn channeled healing light— something the crown showed her instinctively—and felt the power flow from her into him. The wound closed partially, enough to fight on but not fully healed.

The drain on her power was severe. She'd used too much too fast.

Pace yourself, the crown warned. *You cannot win through single overwhelming attacks. This is a battle of endurance.*

Kira proved the crown right. While the lieutenant was focused on Brynn and Thomas, she'd circled behind it, climbing onto a fallen log for height. Now she leaped, landing on the creature's back and driving her sword down with both hands.

The blade sank deep between the lieutenant's shoulder blades. It screamed, bucking like a wild horse, but Kira held on, working the blade deeper.

"Now!" Kira shouted. "While it's distracted!"

Brynn and Thomas struck together—Thomas at the legs, his sword cutting tendons, and Brynn with another beam of light aimed at the wound Kira had opened. The concentrated power burned into the lieutenant's core.

For a moment, Brynn thought they'd won.

Then the lieutenant's body exploded outward into shadow.

Kira was thrown clear, landing hard twenty feet away. Thomas stumbled backward, temporarily blinded by the sudden darkness. And Brynn found herself standing in the center of a sphere of absolute black, unable to see, unable to sense anything except the lieutenant's voice surrounding her.

"Did you think it would be that easy? Did you think a lieutenant of the Shadow Court would fall to simple steel and untrained light?"

Something struck Brynn from behind, driving her to her knees. Then from the side. Then from above. The lieutenant was everywhere and nowhere, attacking from the darkness itself.

Focus, the crown commanded. *You know what to do. Remember what you are.*

Brynn closed her eyes—useless in the darkness anyway—and reached inward instead of outward. Felt the crown's power coiled inside her like a spring. Felt her own heartbeat, steady despite the pain. Felt the bond with Thomas and Kira, still alive, still fighting somewhere beyond the darkness.

She wasn't alone. She'd never been alone.

"Together," Brynn whispered.

And she released everything.

Light exploded from her in all directions—not controlled, not aimed, just pure radiance flooding outward until the darkness couldn't contain it. The sphere shattered, and Brynn saw the lieutenant clearly now, its form halfway between stag and shadow, vulnerable as it transitioned between states.

Thomas was there, sword raised. Kira was there, already running forward despite her injuries. And Brynn channeled the last of her strength into one final strike.

Three attacks hit simultaneously.

Thomas's sword through the chest. Kira's blade across the throat. And Brynn's light burning through from the inside out.

The lieutenant froze, its many eyes wide with something that might have been surprise. It tried to speak, but only darkness leaked from its mouth.

Then it fell, collapsing into ash that blew away on a wind that smelled of burnt corruption.

Brynn collapsed too, exhausted beyond measure, the crown's glow dimming to almost nothing. She'd given everything. Used every drop of power she could channel. If another enemy appeared now, she'd have no defense.

But the forest was silent.

Slowly, impossibly, color began to return. The blackened bark lightened to brown. The twisted branches straightened. The copper taste in the air faded to something cleaner.

"The breach," Kira said, pointing.

The tear in reality was closing. Not completely—Brynn could still see darkness beyond it—but shrinking, the edges knitting together like a wound beginning to heal.

You did not seal it permanently, the crown said. *That knowledge is still locked from you. But you weakened it. Bought time. Delayed the inevitable.*

"How long?" Brynn asked aloud.

Weeks. Perhaps a month before it grows this strong again.

Not enough time. Not nearly enough. But better than nothing.

Thomas helped Brynn to her feet, and she immediately checked him over. His leg wound had reopened during the fight, and he had other injuries she hadn't seen—claw marks across his back, a deep bruise on his ribs that suggested a broken bone.

"I'm fine," he protested as she channeled the last dregs of her power into healing him.

"You're not," Brynn said. "But you will be. Just... stop being so heroic for a few minutes."

"I'll try," Thomas said with a weak smile.

Kira was in better shape, just bruised and scraped from being thrown clear. She stood at the edge of the clearing, staring at the slowly healing forest.

"Is it always like this?" she asked quietly. "This... terrible?"

"I think so," Brynn admitted, joining her. "This is what being a guardian means. Fighting battles like this, over and over, to protect people who'll never know we were here."

"Sounds exhausting."

"It is."

They stood together, watching the forest slowly return to something resembling normal. The corrupted animals had fled or died when the lieutenant fell. Birds were already returning—real birds, with normal feathers and single heads.

"We need to move," Thomas said, though he winced as he said it. "That fight wasn't exactly quiet. If there are people nearby, they'll investigate."

He was right. The battle had been loud, destructive, impossible to miss. And Brynn didn't want to explain why they'd been fighting a monster from nightmare in the middle of a corrupting forest.

They gathered their scattered supplies and headed south, away from the healing breach. The going was slow—all three of them were injured and exhausted—but they pushed on until they found another of those ancient marker stones.

This one was cracked, its wards nearly spent, but it would hold for one night.

They made camp, ate sparingly from their dwindling supplies, and tended to their wounds properly. Brynn tried to heal Thomas further, but the crown had nothing left to give. She'd used it all in the fight.

"How long until you recover?" Kira asked.

Brynn reached inward, assessing. "A day, maybe two, before I can use the crown's power again without hurting myself. Longer to fully recover."

"And we have to do that two more times," Thomas said, not quite a question.

"Two more," Brynn confirmed. "That was the weakest lieutenant. The next two will be harder."

They sat in heavy silence, the weight of what lay ahead pressing down on them.

"Tell me about Thornhaven," Kira said suddenly. "About home. What's it like?"

Thomas smiled slightly. "Small. Quiet. Everyone knows everyone. The kind of place where your biggest worry is whether Mrs. Henderson's pie will win the summer festival again."

"It sounds nice," Kira said wistfully.

"It is," Brynn agreed. "Or it was. I don't know what we'll find when we go back."

"We'll find it standing," Thomas said firmly. "Because that's the next breach we seal. We protect home."

Brynn wanted to share his certainty, but she'd felt the second breach through the crown's awareness. It was stronger than this one had been. The lieutenant there commanded not just beasts but corrupted people—humans twisted by shadow into weapons.

Fighting monsters was one thing. Fighting people, even corrupted ones, was another.

But that was a problem for later. Right now, they needed rest.

They set watches—unnecessarily, probably, given the warding stone, but habits kept them alive. Brynn took last watch, sitting in the pre-dawn darkness and thinking about everything that had happened.

They'd won. Barely, desperately, at tremendous cost, but they'd won. The first lieutenant was defeated, the first breach weakened.

Two more to go.

The crown stirred against her thoughts. *You did well,* it said, and the approval in its voice was genuine. *Better than many guardians on their first true battle. You learned quickly, adapted when overwhelmed, trusted your companions.*

"I nearly got us killed," Brynn said. "I used too much power too fast. Left myself vulnerable."

Yes, the crown agreed. *And you survived anyway. You learned. That is what matters. A guardian who never makes mistakes is a guardian who never takes risks. And without risks, the balance cannot be maintained.*

"The next fight will be harder," Brynn said.

Yes.

"And the one after that harder still."

Yes.

"What if I'm not strong enough? What if I fail?"

The crown was silent for a long moment. Then: *Then you fail. And someone else takes up the burden. And they try where you could not. That is how it has always been. That is how it will always be.*

Oddly, the honesty was comforting. The crown didn't promise victory. Didn't guarantee success. It just acknowledged reality and trusted her to do her best within it.

She could work with that.

Dawn came slowly, painting the forest in shades of gold and green. Real colors, not the sickly corruption that had tainted everything before. They'd done that. Their fight had made this possible.

Thomas and Kira woke, and they shared a quiet breakfast. No one spoke much—they were all processing what they'd been through, preparing mentally for what came next.

"We head south," Brynn said finally. "Back toward civilization. We need proper rest, proper food, time to heal before we attempt the second breach."

"How long?" Kira asked.

"A week. Maybe two if we can afford it."

"We can't afford it," Thomas said. "Every day we delay, the breaches grow stronger."

"Every day we rush forward unprepared increases the chance we fail completely," Brynn countered. "The lieutenant at Thornhaven is stronger. We need to be ready."

They compromised on ten days—enough to heal and resupply, not so long that the breaches would grow critical. They'd head for the nearest large town, rest properly, and then approach Thornhaven from the west, giving them a chance to scout the breach before engaging.

It was a plan. Not a great plan, but better than rushing in blind.

They walked south through the healing forest, and with each step, Brynn felt a tiny bit of her strength returning. Not much, but enough to know she'd recover. Given time.

Around midday, they emerged from the forest into farmland. Fields of wheat stretched toward a town visible in the distance—larger than Millbrook, with walls and proper gates.

They came upon a town marked by a weathered sign: "Crossroads - Est. 1203." Thomas studied it. "Market town. We can resupply here, maybe find better armor."

They entered Crossroads looking like exactly what they were—adventurers who'd been through a battle. No one questioned them. Towns this close to the wild lands saw plenty of people who fought monsters for coin.

They found an inn, paid for rooms and baths, and let themselves finally, truly rest.

Brynn soaked in a hot bath, washing away blood and dirt and exhaustion, and let herself feel the victory. They'd won the first battle. Defeated the first lieutenant. Weakened the first breach.

They could do this. It would be hard, dangerous, possibly fatal. But they could do it.

She dressed in clean clothes, adjusted the crown so it sat comfortably—no longer bothering to hide it now that word of the guardian had spread—and went downstairs to find her companions.

Thomas and Kira sat at a corner table, already eating. Real food—hot stew, fresh bread, vegetables that hadn't been dried and preserved. They looked up as she approached, and she saw it in their faces.

They believed in her. Trusted her. Would follow her into the next battle and the one after that, no matter how dangerous.

She couldn't let them down.

"To the first victory," Thomas said, raising his cup.

"To the first victory," Brynn and Kira echoed.

They drank, ate, and began planning for what came next.

The second breach. The second lieutenant. Thornhaven.

Home.

Chapter 14: Lucian's Return

The eighth day in Crossroads dawned gray and cold, with rain drumming against the inn's windows. Brynn woke feeling stronger than she had since the battle—the crown's glow was bright again, her power fully restored, and the lingering aches from her injuries had finally faded.

She found Thomas and Kira already awake, sitting in the common room with steaming mugs of tea and serious expressions.

"What's wrong?" Brynn asked, sliding into a chair beside them.

"Rumor," Kira said quietly. "One of the farmers who came to market yesterday. He said there's a dying man on the road north, asking for the 'new guardian.'"

Brynn's stomach dropped. "Lucian."

"That's what we thought," Thomas confirmed. "The description matches—older man, injured leg, looking half-dead. He's holed up in an abandoned barn about three miles out."

"It could be a trap," Kira warned. "The Shadow Court knows you're hunting their breaches. They could be using him as bait."

Brynn closed her eyes, reaching out with the crown's awareness. She felt the direction Kira indicated, and yes—there was something there. A flicker of magic, faint but familiar. Lucian's signature.

"It's really him," she said. "And he's dying. I can feel it."

Thomas stood immediately. "Then we go. Whatever our history with him, we don't leave him to die alone."

They gathered their gear and headed north on foot, walking carefully on roads turned treacherous by recent rain. The rain had softened to a drizzle by the time they reached the barn—a sagging structure that looked abandoned for years, its roof half-collapsed and walls weathered to gray.

Brynn pushed open the door carefully, hand on her sword.

Lucian lay in the far corner, wrapped in a tattered cloak, and he looked worse than dying. The dark veins that had crawled up his neck now covered half his face. His skin was gray, his breathing shallow, and the leg that had been splinted was twisted at an unnatural angle.

But he was conscious. His eyes opened when they entered, and a weak smile crossed his face.

"You came," he said, his voice barely a whisper. "I wasn't sure you would. Not after I challenged you."

Brynn knelt beside him, and the crown showed her immediately what she already knew—he was beyond healing. The magic that had transported him to the Crystal Valley had extracted a price too high. His life force was burned out, his body failing organ by organ.

Days at most. Maybe hours.

"Why did you come here?" Brynn asked gently. "You could have stayed in the mountains. Died somewhere peaceful."

"Because I have information," Lucian said. "About the breaches. About what's coming. And because..." He coughed, and blood flecked his lips. "Because I wanted to help. One more time. To make up for what I tried to do."

Thomas crouched on Lucian's other side. "Then tell us. Whatever you know."

Lucian's hand fumbled in his cloak and pulled out a leather journal—old, worn, filled with cramped writing. "Twenty years of study. Everything I learned about the Shadow Court, the breaches, the lieutenants. It's yours now. Use it."

Brynn took the journal carefully. Even through leather, she could feel the knowledge it contained. Lucian had spent two decades researching, and he was giving it all away.

"The second lieutenant," Lucian said urgently. "The one near Thornhaven. It's not like the first. It doesn't fight directly. It corrupts. Slowly. Subtly. It turns people against each other, makes them into weapons without them even knowing."

"How do we fight that?" Kira asked.

"Carefully. Watchfully. Trust no one completely until you're certain they're uncorrupted. And seal the breach fast—every day you delay, more people fall under its influence." Lucian coughed again, harder. "There's a spell. In the journal. Page forty-seven. It creates a circle of protection. Anyone inside it can't be corrupted. Use it to protect Thornhaven's core. The people you absolutely cannot afford to lose."

"Thank you," Brynn said, meaning it. Whatever their past conflict, Lucian was trying to help now. That mattered.

"Don't thank me yet." Lucian's grip tightened on her wrist, surprisingly strong for someone so close to death. "The third breach. The Shadow King. Brynn, he knows you're coming. He's not waiting passively like the others. He's preparing. Building an army. By the time you reach him, you'll face not just shadow beasts but organized forces. A real war."

"Then we'll bring an army of our own," Thomas said.

"With what forces?" Lucian challenged. "Thornhaven has forty people who can hold a pitchfork, maybe ten who can actually fight. The other villages nearby are the same. The Shadow King commands thousands."

"We'll find a way," Brynn said firmly.

Lucian studied her face, and something like pride flickered in his dying eyes. "You will. Your grandmother chose well. Better than I ever could admit." His breathing was getting shallower, each word costing him. "One more thing. A name. In my journal. Page ninety-three. A mage I knew, years ago. She owed me a favor. Use my name. She'll help you."

"Rest now," Brynn said, but Lucian shook his head.

"No time. Listen. The Shadow Court... they're not just evil for evil's sake. They're order taken too far. Perfect stasis. No change, no growth, no death but also no life. They see chaos as disease. They think they're healing reality by freezing it."

He coughed again, and this time he didn't stop for nearly a minute. When he finally did, there was more blood.

"The balance," he gasped. "That's why the crown exists. To prevent either extreme. Too much order becomes the Shadow Court. Too much chaos becomes..." He struggled for words. "Something worse. Something that might come after, if you fail."

"We won't fail," Brynn promised.

"No." Lucian's smile was genuine now. "You won't. Because you understand what I never did. The crown isn't about power. It's about service. About sacrifice. About carrying a burden you never wanted because someone has to."

His eyes began to close, his breathing slowing.

"Lucian," Brynn said urgently. "Is there anything we can do? Any way to ease this?"

"You already have," he whispered. "You came. You listened. You gave meaning to my death that my life never had. That's enough."

He took three more shallow breaths, then stopped.

The dark veins faded from his skin, leaving him looking almost peaceful. Almost young again, the way he must have looked before tragedy broke him.

Thomas reached over and gently closed Lucian's eyes. "He deserved better than what he got."

"He got what he chose," Kira said, not unkindly. "And in the end, he chose to help. That counts for something."

They buried him outside the barn, in a grove of oak trees that seemed less touched by the world's corruption. Brynn spoke words over the grave—not formal prayers, just thanks for his help and hopes that he'd found whatever peace he'd been seeking.

As they turned to leave, Brynn opened Lucian's journal to page forty-seven.

The protection spell was there, exactly as he'd said. Complex but clear, with diagrams and notes in Lucian's precise handwriting. It would take time to cast, and she'd need materials—salt, silver, and blood freely given—but it was doable.

She flipped to page ninety-three.

A name was written there in larger script: "Vera Blackthorne. Fire mage. Lives in the Ashwood Mountains, three days east of the Shadow Peaks. Tell her Lucian sent you. Tell her it's time to pay her debt."

Below that, more notes: "Vera is difficult. Proud. Absolutely does not suffer fools. But she's powerful, and she understands the stakes. If anyone can help you raise an army of mages, it's her."

An army of mages. Against the Shadow King's thousands.

It wasn't impossible. Just incredibly difficult.

"We have new plans to make," Brynn said, closing the journal carefully.

They walked back to Crossroads in silence, each processing what they'd learned. By the time they reached the inn, rain had started again—harder now, washing the world clean.

That night, they spread Lucian's journal across their table and read through it carefully. Twenty years of research filled those pages—information about the Shadow Court's history, tactics, weaknesses. Descriptions of the three lieutenants in detail. Theories about how to permanently seal the breaches, not just weaken them.

"Listen to this," Thomas said, reading from a page near the middle. "The lieutenants are connected to their breaches. If you kill the lieutenant before sealing the breach, the breach grows stronger temporarily, feeding on the lieutenant's death. But if you seal the breach first, the lieutenant is cut off from the Shadow Court's power, making it weaker."

"So we've been doing it backward," Brynn said. "We should seal first, fight second."

"But you can't seal the breaches yet," Kira pointed out. "The crown hasn't given you that knowledge."

Brynn touched the crown thoughtfully. "Maybe defeating the first lieutenant was the first step. Maybe each victory unlocks more knowledge. Let me check."

She closed her eyes and reached inward, toward the crown's reservoir of locked knowledge. And yes—something had shifted. There was new information available, just at the edge of her awareness.

She pulled at it gently, and knowledge flooded in.

Sealing rituals. Complex but clear. She'd need time, materials, and perfect concentration. But she could do it now. The crown had judged her ready.

"I can seal them," Brynn said, opening her eyes. "The crown just taught me how. But Lucian was right—it takes time. Twenty minutes of uninterrupted casting. If we're under attack, I won't be able to complete it."

"Then we need a plan," Thomas said. "For Thornhaven. We scout the breach first. Find the lieutenant. Then two of us distract it while you seal the breach. Once it's sealed, we fight the weakened lieutenant together."

"Simple," Kira said. "Probably won't work. But it's better than nothing."

They spent two more days in Crossroads, studying Lucian's journal and preparing. Brynn memorized the sealing ritual until she could recite it in her sleep. Thomas and Kira practiced fighting together, learning each other's rhythms and signals.

On the morning of the tenth day, they set out toward Thornhaven.

The journey took three days through increasingly familiar territory. Brynn recognized landmarks from her childhood—the lightning-struck oak, the stream with the rope swing, the hill where she'd first kissed Thomas during the summer festival two years ago.

They were coming home.

But as they crested the final hill and looked down at Thornhaven, Brynn's heart sank.

The village looked wrong. Not corrupted, not destroyed, but... diminished. Smaller somehow. The streets were too quiet. Smoke rose from fewer chimneys than there should be. And over everything hung a pall of gray that had nothing to do with weather.

"What happened?" Thomas whispered, horror in his voice.

Brynn reached out with the crown's awareness and felt it immediately. The corruption was here. Not obvious, not visible, but present. Seeping through the village like poison in water.

The second lieutenant was working its influence slowly, subtly, just as Lucian had warned.

"How bad is it?" Kira asked.

"Bad," Brynn said. "Not everyone's affected yet, but enough are that the social fabric is fraying. People are suspicious of each other. Arguments over nothing. Trust breaking down."

"My father," Thomas said suddenly. "My family. Are they—"

"I don't know," Brynn admitted. "We need to go down there. Carefully. Figure out who's still uncorrupted. Protect them before we attempt the breach."

They descended the hill slowly, and with each step, Brynn felt the wrongness intensify. The second lieutenant's power was more insidious than the first. Instead of corrupting the physical world, it corrupted relationships, trust, community.

It was turning Thornhaven against itself.

And Brynn had to stop it before the village tore itself apart.

Chapter 15: Thornhaven Poisoned

They entered Thornhaven from the west, hoods up despite the autumn sun. Better to scout quietly before announcing their return. The village square—usually bustling at midday—was nearly empty. A few people hurried past with heads down, avoiding eye contact. No one called greetings. No one smiled.

"This is wrong," Thomas muttered. "Thornhaven is never this quiet."

A woman Brynn recognized—Mrs. Henderson, the baker—emerged from her shop with flour-dusted hands. She glanced at the three travelers, then her eyes went hard and suspicious.

"Move along," she said sharply. "We don't welcome strangers here."

"Mrs. Henderson, it's me," Thomas said, pulling back his hood. "Thomas Blackwood. You've known me since I was born."

The suspicion didn't fade from her face. Instead, it intensified. "Thomas. Yes. The boy who abandoned his family to run off with that Ashford girl." She spat the name like a curse. "Probably brought trouble with you. Always knew she was bad luck."

Thomas recoiled as if struck. Brynn caught his arm, squeezing gently.

"We're just passing through," Brynn said carefully. "Looking for Thomas's father. Where would we find him?"

Mrs. Henderson hesitated, clearly torn between maintaining her hostility and her lifelong neighborliness. Neighborliness won, barely. "Forge. Where else? But don't expect a warm welcome. Half the village blames your family for the troubles."

"What troubles?" Thomas asked, but Mrs. Henderson had already retreated into her shop, slamming the door.

They exchanged worried glances and headed toward the forge.

The blacksmith's was on the eastern edge of town, and as they approached, Brynn could see the change. The usually immaculate yard was scattered with broken tools and scrap metal. The forge itself still smoked, but the sound of hammering was erratic, angry.

Thomas pushed open the door. "Father?"

A man looked up from the anvil—Thomas's father, but aged years in the month since they'd left.

His face was haggard, his eyes bloodshot, his movements jerky with exhaustion or anger or both.

"Thomas." The word was flat, emotionless. "You came back."

"Of course I came back," Thomas said. "You're my father. This is my home."

"Is it?" His father set down his hammer with deliberate care. "Funny how you remembered that after weeks of abandonment. After leaving me to deal with the rumors, the accusations, the problems."

"What accusations?" Thomas asked, moving closer despite Brynn's warning hand on his arm.

"That you were involved in the disappearances. That you and the Ashford girl were working some dark magic. That you brought a curse to Thornhaven." His father's voice was rising. "People stopped coming to the forge. Orders were canceled. I've lost half my income because my son decided to run off on some fool's quest!"

"That's the corruption talking," Brynn said quietly. She could see it now—dark tendrils wrapped around Thomas's father's mind, twisting his thoughts, amplifying anger and suspicion. "It's not really him."

But Thomas was staring at his father with pain in his eyes. "You don't mean that. You said you understood when I left. You gave me your blessing."

"I was wrong." His father turned back to the anvil, picking up the hammer again. "You should leave. Go back to wherever you've been. Thornhaven doesn't need you anymore."

Thomas stood frozen, and Brynn saw his heart breaking. This was exactly what Lucian had warned about—the lieutenant didn't just corrupt individuals, it corrupted relationships, turning love to suspicion, trust to accusation.

"Come on," Brynn said gently, pulling Thomas toward the door. "This isn't him. We'll fix it, but we need to understand the situation first."

They left the forge and found a quiet spot behind the church—one of the few places that still felt clean. Brynn pulled out Lucian's journal, flipping to the section about corruption detection.

"We need to identify who's still themselves," she said. "The protection spell will save them, but we need to cast it on the right people."

"How do we tell who's corrupted?" Kira asked.

Brynn read through Lucian's notes. "The crown can see it, apparently. I just need to... attune differently. Look at people through the crown's awareness rather than my own eyes."

She closed her eyes and let the crown's perception overlay her own vision. When she opened them again, the world looked different.

Thomas and Kira glowed softly golden—untainted, still themselves. But moving through the streets of Thornhaven were dozens of people wrapped in darkness. Not completely black, but shadowed, their auras murky and twisted.

"About half the village is affected," Brynn reported. "Some worse than others. Mrs. Henderson is lightly touched—she can still be saved easily. Your father..." She hesitated. "He's more deeply corrupted. It's fixable, but it'll take work after we seal the breach."

"Who's still clean?" Thomas asked, his voice tight with control.

Brynn scanned the village through the crown's sight. "The priest. About a dozen others scattered throughout. The children, thank the balance—whatever this lieutenant is doing, it can't or won't touch children."

"Then we protect the priest and the others first," Kira said. "Cast the protection spell on them. Then we go after the breach."

"Where is the breach?" Thomas asked.

Brynn extended her awareness, feeling for the tear in reality. And there—northeast of the village, deep in the forest where she and Thomas had played as children. The old hunting grounds. Maybe half a mile from the village's edge.

"The forest," she said. "The old oak grove."

Thomas's expression darkened. "The Hanging Oak. Where they used to execute criminals, centuries ago. Of course the corruption would anchor there."

They spent the afternoon carefully approaching the still-clean villagers, one by one. The priest was first—a kind old man named Father Benedict who recognized Brynn immediately and listened without interruption as she explained about the corruption.

"I've felt something wrong," he said quietly. "Seen good people turning against each other for no reason. I've been praying for guidance. Are you saying this is an answer to prayer?"

"Or I'm a sign of the apocalypse," Brynn said with a slight smile. "Hard to say. But I can protect you. Keep the corruption from touching your mind. Will you trust me?"

Father Benedict looked at her for a long moment, then at the crown on her head. "You're Aubre's granddaughter. She was one of the finest women I ever knew. If she prepared you for something, then yes. I trust you."

The protection spell required salt, silver, and blood freely given. Brynn had brought salt and silver from Crossroads. The blood had to be hers—guardian's blood was part of what made the spell work.

She drew a circle around Father Benedict with salt, placed silver coins at the cardinal points—borrowed from the priest's own collection—and pricked her finger to let three drops of blood fall at the circle's center. Then she channeled power through the crown and spoke the words Lucian had written.

The spell took five minutes of perfect concentration. When it was complete, a shimmer of light surrounded Father Benedict—invisible to normal sight but clear through the crown's vision. The corruption couldn't touch him now.

"It feels... lighter," Father Benedict said wonderingly. "Like a weight I didn't know I was carrying has lifted."

"You'll stay clear-minded no matter what the lieutenant tries," Brynn explained. "And the corruption can't use you against others. You're safe. But we need to protect more people before we can attempt sealing the breach."

They spent the next two days carefully casting the protection spell on the other clean villagers. It was exhausting work—each casting drained Brynn significantly, and she could only manage four or five per day before needing to rest.

But slowly, they created a core of protected people. Thirteen in total, including Father Benedict. Not much, but it would have to be enough.

On the third night, they made camp in the forest outside Thornhaven, not trusting the village itself. Brynn sat up late, studying Lucian's journal by firelight.

"The lieutenant will be at the breach," she said. "Lucian's notes say it looks human but wrong. Moves wrong. Talks wrong. And it's smart—smarter than the first lieutenant. It'll try to negotiate, to stall, to turn us against each other."

"So we don't listen," Thomas said. "We go in, you seal the breach, we fight. Simple."

"Nothing about this is simple," Brynn countered. "The sealing takes twenty minutes. You and Kira will have to hold the lieutenant off for twenty minutes while I'm completely vulnerable. And it'll do everything in its power to disrupt the casting."

"Then we hold it off," Kira said firmly. "We've done impossible things before."

Brynn wanted to argue, to find some safer plan, but there wasn't one. This was the path forward—dangerous, possibly fatal, but necessary.

"Tomorrow," she said finally. "At dawn. We go to the breach, and we end this."

That night, Brynn barely slept. Every time she closed her eyes, she saw the corrupted faces of Thornhaven's people. Saw Thomas's father, twisted with suspicion. Saw Mrs. Henderson, kind her whole life, turned hostile. Saw the empty streets where children should have been playing.

This lieutenant had taken her home and poisoned it. Made it sick. And she was going to make it pay for that.

Dawn came cold and clear. They broke camp, checked their weapons and armor, and headed toward the old oak grove.

The forest grew darker as they approached the breach. Not corrupted like the first forest had been, but wrong in subtler ways. Trees grew too close together. Shadows fell at impossible angles. And the silence was absolute—no birds, no insects, nothing alive.

They reached the Hanging Oak just as the sun cleared the horizon.

The tree was massive, ancient, its branches twisted from centuries of bearing grim fruit. And at its base, sitting on an old stone that might have once been a judge's seat, was the lieutenant.

It looked almost human. Almost. A woman, beautiful even, with flowing dark hair and eyes that seemed kind. She wore simple clothes—a dress that could have belonged to any Thornhaven villager.

But the shadows around her moved wrong. And when she smiled, her teeth were just slightly too sharp.

"Welcome home, Brynn Thornwick," the lieutenant said, her voice honey-sweet and poisonous. "Shall we talk about what you've done to my village?"

Chapter 16: The Lieutenant Of Lies

The lieutenant stood gracefully, and Brynn noticed how the shadows clung to her like a living cloak. Through the crown's vision, she could see the corruption radiating from the woman in waves—not violent like the first lieutenant's power, but insidious, seeping into everything it touched.

"Welcome home, Brynn Thornwick," the lieutenant said, her voice honey-sweet and poisonous. "I've been tending to your village in your absence."

"Your village?" Brynn said, keeping her voice steady. "Thornhaven belongs to the people who live there."

The lieutenant laughed, and it sounded genuinely amused. "Does it?

Look at them now—suspicious, afraid, turning against each other. I've shown them their true nature. All that neighborly kindness was just a pleasant lie hiding the truth."

"That's not true," Thomas said, his hand on his sword hilt.

"Isn't it?" The lieutenant's gaze fixed on him. "Your father thinks you abandoned him. Do you think that suspicion came from nowhere? Or did I simply amplify what was already there—his fear that you'd leave him like your mother did?"

Thomas flinched, and Brynn saw the words hit home. His mother had died when he was young, and his father had raised him alone. The fear of abandonment would have been there, buried deep.

"Don't listen to her," Brynn said. "That's what she does. She takes truth and twists it into poison."

"Oh, I like that," the lieutenant said. "Truth twisted into poison. Yes. That's exactly what I am. But here's the thing, little guardian—all poison starts as medicine. All lies start as truth. I don't create the suspicions and fears. I just make them impossible to ignore."

Kira had been circling quietly during this exchange, positioning herself behind the lieutenant. But the corrupted woman didn't seem concerned.

"Your translator friend is wondering if she can stab me while I'm distracted," the lieutenant said without turning around. "The answer is yes. The question is whether it will help. I'm not like my brother in the Corrupted Forest. I don't need this body to exist. Kill me here, and I'll just reform somewhere else in the village. Unless..."

She smiled, and it was terrible in its gentleness.

"Unless you seal the breach first. Cut me off from the Shadow Court. That would hurt. That would actually threaten me. But you need twenty minutes to cast the sealing ritual, don't you? And I don't think your friends can keep me occupied that long."

"Try us," Thomas said, drawing his sword.

The lieutenant sighed. "So aggressive. So quick to violence. Is it any wonder your father fears you? Fears what you might become in the company of this girl?" She gestured at Brynn. "She wears a crown of power and claims it's for balance. But power always corrupts. Always. Give her ten years, and she'll be worse than the Shadow Court ever was."

"You're stalling," Brynn said, recognizing the tactic. Every word the lieutenant spoke was designed to create doubt, to wedge cracks into their unity. "Trying to delay us while the breach grows stronger."

"Am I? Or am I trying to save you? The Shadow Court isn't evil, child. We're order. Structure. The end of chaos and suffering. Let the breach open completely. Let us remake your world into something better. No more pain. No more betrayal. No more lies."

"Just eternal stasis," Brynn said. "Everyone frozen in place, no growth, no change, no life. Lucian told me what you really are."

The lieutenant's pleasant expression flickered for just a moment. "Lucian. Poor broken Lucian. He understood us better than anyone. We could have saved him, you know. Frozen him in a moment before his guilt, before his pain. Let him live forever in happiness. But he chose suffering instead. How very human."

"He chose to stay human," Brynn corrected. "To feel pain and guilt because that's what being alive means. Now—" she drew her own sword, channeled power through the crown until it blazed with light, "—I'm going to seal your breach. And you're going to try to stop me. Let's not pretend this ends any other way."

The lieutenant's smile widened. "Oh, I knew I liked you. Yes. Let's not pretend. But know this—I won't just try to kill you. I'll make you kill each other. I'll twist every doubt, every fear, every buried resentment until you're tearing each other apart. And you'll do it believing you're doing the right thing."

She raised one hand, and darkness exploded from her palm.

Not physical darkness—emotional darkness. Brynn felt it slam into her mind like a wave, carrying with it every doubt she'd ever had about herself, her mission, her companions. The crown burned bright, pushing it back, but she felt the edges of it seeping through.

Thomas and Kira weren't so protected.

Thomas stumbled, his sword drooping, and when he looked at Brynn his eyes were full of uncertainty. "Is she right? Will the crown corrupt you? Will I watch you become a monster?"

"Thomas, no," Brynn said, but she could see the lieutenant's power working on him, amplifying his deepest fear—that he'd follow Brynn into darkness and lose himself in the process.

Kira had dropped to one knee, trembling. "I don't belong here," she whispered. "I'm just a translator. What am I doing fighting monsters? I'm going to get them killed. I'm going to fail them when they need me most."

"Kira, stand up," Brynn commanded, but the woman didn't move, trapped in her own spiral of self-doubt.

The lieutenant laughed. "See how easy? They want to believe the worst about themselves. Everyone does. I just help them see it."

Brynn channeled power through the crown, creating a shield around her companions. The emotional darkness pushed back against it, but slowly, Thomas and Kira's eyes cleared.

"Sorry," Thomas said, shaking his head. "That was... awful. Felt real."

"It was real," the lieutenant said. "Those are your true fears. Your true doubts. I didn't invent them. I just made you face them."

"Then we face them," Brynn said. "Together. Thomas, Kira—I need you to hold her off. Twenty minutes. Can you do it?"

Thomas steadied himself, raised his sword. "Yes."

"Absolutely," Kira said, though she still looked shaken.

Brynn moved toward the breach—a tear in reality barely visible behind the Hanging Oak, darkness leaking through like blood from a wound. She'd need to cast the sealing right at the breach's edge, vulnerable to attack, unable to defend herself while the magic worked.

"Now," she said.

Thomas and Kira attacked simultaneously.

The lieutenant didn't draw a weapon. She didn't need to. Shadow formed around her hands like claws, and she met Thomas's sword with darkness that shouldn't have been solid but was. The blade passed through shadow and hit nothing.

"You can't cut doubt," the lieutenant said, almost sadly. "Can't stab fear. I'm not really here, boy. I'm in your mind. In everyone's mind. Killing my body changes nothing."

But Kira had circled behind and struck low, her blade cutting through the lieutenant's leg. Dark ichor flowed—the same substance that had bled from the first lieutenant. The lieutenant shrieked and stumbled.

"Seems pretty real to me," Kira said.

Brynn reached the breach and began the ritual. She drew a circle with salt, placed silver coins at the compass points, and pricked her palm to let blood flow freely. Then she began chanting the words Lucian had written, channeling power through the crown in a specific pattern.

The sealing was complex. Each phrase had to be perfect, each gesture exact. One mistake and she'd have to start over. And she was completely defenseless while casting—all her concentration devoted to the ritual, none left for protection.

Behind her, Thomas and Kira fought desperately.

The lieutenant was fast, impossibly fast, and every strike she landed carried her poison. Thomas blocked a blow and immediately had to fight off a vision of Brynn dying because he'd been too slow. Kira dodged and found herself seeing her own funeral, attended by no one because she'd died forgotten and alone.

But they kept fighting. Kept pushing back. Kept the lieutenant away from Brynn.

Five minutes passed. Ten.

The lieutenant changed tactics. If she couldn't break through Thomas and Kira physically, she'd break them mentally.

"Thomas," she said, her voice soft. "Your father will never forgive you. No matter how many villages you save, no matter how many breaches you seal, he'll always see you as the son who abandoned him. Is that really worth it?"

Thomas's sword wavered. "Brynn," he called without turning. "Is she right? Will my father hate me forever?"

Brynn wanted to answer but couldn't break her concentration. The ritual demanded everything she had.

"She's not right," Kira said, covering for her. "The corruption will fade when the breach is sealed. He'll remember who he really is."

"Will he?" the lieutenant pressed. "Or was the corruption just revealing what was always there? The resentment. The feeling of being second choice. The knowledge that his son loved a girl more than he loved his father."

"Stop," Thomas said, but his voice was weak.

Fifteen minutes.

The lieutenant turned to Kira. "And you, translator. How many people have you translated for? How many languages do you speak? But do you remember your mother's voice? Your father's face? You've been running so long from who you were that you've become nothing. Just an echo of other people's words."

Kira's hands shook on her sword. "That's not true."

"Isn't it? Name one thing you want. One thing that's yours, not borrowed, not translated, not a reflection of someone else's desire. You can't. You're empty inside. And you know it."

Kira's stance wavered. For a moment, Brynn thought she might drop her sword entirely. But then something shifted in the woman's expression.

"You're right," Kira said quietly. "I don't know what I want. I've spent so long being useful to others that I forgot to be someone for myself. But you know what I just figured out?"

She attacked, her sword moving in a pattern that surprised even the lieutenant.

"I want to be someone who stops monsters like you. That's mine. That's my choice. And it's enough."

The blade struck true, sinking deep into the lieutenant's chest. Dark ichor flowed, and the lieutenant gasped—actually hurt, actually vulnerable for the first time in the fight.

"Clever," she hissed. "But not clever enough."

She grabbed Kira's sword hand, and darkness poured from her touch. Kira screamed as the lieutenant's full power slammed into her mind— every doubt, every fear, every moment of weakness amplified a thousand fold.

Thomas rushed to help, but the lieutenant's other hand caught his throat. "Let's see everything you fear, shall we? Let me show you all the ways you're going to fail."

Eighteen minutes.

Brynn could feel them breaking. Could sense Thomas and Kira's will crumbling under the lieutenant's assault. Two more minutes and the ritual would be complete. Just two more minutes.

But her friends would be destroyed by then.

She had to choose. Break the ritual to save them, or complete the sealing and risk losing them forever to the lieutenant's poison.

The crown weighed heavy on her head, and she knew what it would counsel. The balance required sacrifice. The many over the few. Complete the sealing. Protect Thornhaven. Let Thomas and Kira pay the price if necessary.

That's what a guardian would do.

Brynn kept chanting. Kept channeling power into the ritual. While behind her, Thomas and Kira screamed.

I'm sorry, she thought to them. *I'm so sorry.*

Nineteen minutes.

The lieutenant's laughter echoed through the grove. "Yes! This is what it means to be a guardian! To sacrifice everything, everyone, for the greater good! Welcome to your first real decision, little crown-bearer. Welcome to learning what it costs."

Thirty seconds remaining.

Thomas had fallen to his knees, hands pressed to his head, trying to block out the visions the lieutenant was forcing into his mind. Kira lay on the ground, curled in a ball, sobbing.

The lieutenant stood over them, triumphant. "And you'll live with this. Forever. Knowing you could have saved them but chose the mission instead. That's the burden you carry now. That's what it means to serve the balance."

Twenty seconds.

Please, Brynn thought desperately. *Please let them survive this. Please let it not be permanent.*

Ten seconds.

The lieutenant raised both hands, darkness gathering for a final strike that would shatter Thomas and Kira's minds completely.

Five seconds.

Brynn spoke the final words of the ritual, released the last of her power into the spell, and felt it snap into place.

The breach sealed.

Not perfectly, not permanently, but enough. The flow of corruption stopped. The lieutenant's connection to the Shadow Court severed.

The darkness around the lieutenant guttered like a candle flame in wind. She looked down at her hands in shock.

"No," she whispered. "No, you actually did it. You actually sacrificed them for—"

Thomas's sword took her through the heart.

He'd risen while she was distracted, moved while she was weakened. And now his blade pierced her fully, pinning her to the Hanging Oak.

"Wrong," Thomas said, his voice rough but steady. "She didn't sacrifice us. She trusted us to hold. And we did."

The lieutenant looked down at the sword, then at Thomas, then at Brynn who had collapsed after finishing the ritual. "Clever. All of you. Cleverer than I gave you credit for."

She smiled, and for the first time it looked genuine. Almost peaceful.

"The corruption will fade now. The breach is sealed. You've won this battle, little guardian. But know this—my siblings are stronger. The Corrupted Forest was weakest. Thornhaven was second. But the Shadow Peaks..." She coughed, and darkness leaked from her mouth. "The Shadow King has been preparing for a century. You can't beat him. No one can."

"We'll find a way," Brynn said.

"Yes." The lieutenant was fading now, her form becoming translucent. "You probably will. That's what makes you dangerous. You never know when to give up."

She dissolved into shadow and was gone. All that remained was Thomas's sword, driven deep into the oak's trunk.

Thomas pulled it free and immediately went to Kira, who was still curled on the ground. "Kira. Hey. It's over. We won."

Kira uncurled slowly, her face tear-streaked but aware. "Did we? I feel like I just had my entire soul turned inside out."

"Yeah," Thomas said. "But you're still here. Still you. That's what matters."

Brynn tried to stand and couldn't. She'd given everything to the sealing, had nothing left. Thomas helped her to her feet, supporting her weight.

"You actually kept casting," he said quietly. "Even while we were breaking. You trusted us to hold."

"I didn't have a choice," Brynn admitted. "The ritual couldn't be interrupted."

"You had a choice," Thomas corrected. "You could have broken the ritual to save us. You chose to trust instead. That's..." He smiled slightly. "That's what makes you a good guardian."

They left the grove slowly, exhausted beyond measure. As they emerged from the forest, they saw people emerging from their homes—Thornhaven's villagers, looking around in confusion as if waking from a bad dream.

The corruption was fading. The lieutenant's death had severed it, and with the breach sealed, no new poison flowed in. People would recover. Relationships would mend. The village would heal.

Thomas's father was one of the first they encountered. He saw Thomas and stopped, confusion crossing his face.

"Thomas? I... I said terrible things to you. I don't know why. I felt so angry, so suspicious, but I can't remember why." He looked lost. "What happened to me?"

"Something bad," Thomas said. "But it's over now. You're yourself again."

They embraced, and Brynn looked away, giving them privacy for their reunion.

Thornhaven was saved.

Two breaches sealed. Two lieutenants defeated.

One more to go.

Chapter 17: Preparing For War

Three days after sealing the Thornhaven breach, Brynn stood in her grandmother's garden and finally let herself fall apart.

She'd held together through the lieutenant's defeat, through helping the corrupted villagers recover, through a dozen tearful reunions as families remembered themselves. She'd been strong, steady, the guardian everyone needed her to be.

But now, alone in the quiet garden where her grandmother had told her stories by moonlight, she collapsed onto the bench and sobbed.

For Lucian, who'd died alone trying to help. For Thomas's father and the days lost to corruption. For every person in Thornhaven who'd hurt someone they loved while poisoned by the lieutenant's touch. For the weight of what still lay ahead—one more breach, one more lieutenant, and this one stronger than both the others combined.

She cried until she had nothing left, until the grief and fear and exhaustion emptied out and left her hollow.

"That's healthy," a voice said.

Brynn looked up to find Father Benedict standing at the garden gate, his weathered face kind. "Most people who carry weight like yours never let themselves cry. Then it builds up until they break."

"I can't afford to break," Brynn said.

"Everyone can afford to break in private," Father Benedict replied, settling onto the bench beside her. "It's breaking in public that's dangerous." He was quiet for a moment. "Your grandmother used to sit here too. Did you know that? After your grandfather died, she'd come out here at night and cry where no one could see. Then she'd go inside, dry her eyes, and be strong for your mother. For the village. For everyone who needed her."

"She walked away from the crown," Brynn said. "Did she ever regret it?"

"Every day," Father Benedict said honestly. "But she never regretted you. She'd look at you playing in this garden and say, 'She'll be ready. When the time comes, she'll do what I couldn't.' And she was right."

Brynn wiped her eyes. "Two down. One to go."

"The Shadow King," Father Benedict said. "Everyone's talking about him. About the Shadow Peaks. About what you'll face there."

"It's going to be war," Brynn said. "Not a battle. An actual war. The Shadow King has armies. Thousands of corrupted creatures and shadow warriors. Lucian's journal says he's been building them for decades, preparing for the moment the prison fails."

"Then you'll need an army too," Father Benedict said.

"With what forces? Thornhaven has maybe fifty people who can hold weapons, and half of them just recovered from corruption. The other villages nearby are the same or worse." Brynn shook her head. "We're going to lose."

"Not necessarily." Father Benedict pulled a folded letter from his robe. "This came for you. A runner brought it from Crossroads yesterday."

Brynn unfolded the letter and recognized the handwriting immediately—Kira's, written in the neat script of someone trained to copy manuscripts.

Brynn—

I've been asking around about mages. About people who might help with the Shadow Peaks. Turns out there's a whole network of them, scattered throughout the region. Most are solitary, but they communicate. Share information.

I sent out messages to thirty-seven different mages, explaining the situation. Explaining what we're facing and what's at stake.

Twelve have responded so far. Eight are willing to help. That's not an army, but it's a start.

Also—Thomas has been talking to his father's contacts. Other blacksmiths, merchants who travel the region, village leaders. Word is spreading. People are scared of the Shadow Court. Scared enough to want to do something about it.

We might be able to raise a real force. Not huge, but enough.

Meet us at the Crossroads inn tomorrow evening. We have things to discuss.

—K

Brynn read the letter twice, hope kindling in her chest. "They're raising an army."

"Your friends are remarkable," Father Benedict observed. "Most people would have fled after what you all went through. They're doubling down instead."

"I need to go," Brynn said, standing. "If they're gathering forces, I need to be there. Need to convince people this matters."

"It's a three-day walk to Crossroads," Father Benedict said. "But I think young Marcus has a horse he'd lend you. Might get there in a day and a half if you push."

Brynn hugged the old priest impulsively. "Thank you. For everything. For staying sane while the village lost its mind. For being here now."

"Thank your grandmother," Father Benedict said. "She taught me to see past the surface. To trust in things I couldn't prove. You're proof her faith was justified."

Brynn borrowed Marcus's horse—a sturdy mare used to hard travel—and rode east. The crown had grown lighter over the past days, or maybe she'd just grown stronger. Its weight no longer pressed on her head but rested there comfortably, part of her now.

She reached Crossroads by noon the next day, returned the horse to Marcus's cousin who lived there, and found her way to the inn.

Thomas and Kira sat at a large table covered in maps and lists, surrounded by a dozen people Brynn didn't recognize. The conversation stopped when she entered.

"Everyone," Thomas said, standing. "This is Brynn Thornwick:. The guardian."

Brynn expected skepticism, disbelief, demands for proof. Instead, the gathered people simply studied her—taking in the crown, the armor she still wore, the way power radiated from her even at rest.

"You sealed two breaches," a woman said—older, with silver hair and scars across her hands that suggested a lifetime of working with dangerous magic. "Killed two lieutenants. That's more than any guardian has accomplished in a century."

"You're Vera Blackthorne," Brynn said, recognizing her from Lucian's description. "Lucian said you owed him a debt."

Vera's expression flickered. "Lucian is dead. I felt it three weeks ago when his magic finally guttered out. Whatever debt I owed him, I can't repay."

"He said to tell you it's time," Brynn said. "Time to pay what you owed by helping me. By raising mages to fight the Shadow King."

Vera was silent for a long moment, then nodded slowly. "Lucian saved my life forty years ago. Pulled me from a burning building and nearly died doing it. I swore I'd pay that debt someday." She gestured to the maps. "Consider it paid. I've brought seven other mages. We're yours to command."

"Eight mages," said a young man with nervous energy. "Counting me. Fire magic, mostly. Some shielding."

Others introduced themselves—earth mages, water mages, one woman who specialized in illusions and another who could heal. Not a large force, but skilled. Powerful. More than Brynn had dared hope for.

"That's the magic," Thomas said. "Now for the fighters."

He gestured to another group—village leaders and merchants, people with resources and connections. "We've spread word through the merchant networks. The Shadow Court threatens everyone, not just Thornhaven. Other villages want to help. They're sending fighters—not many per village, but added together it becomes significant."

"How many?" Brynn asked.

"Two hundred," Thomas said. "Maybe two-fifty if we push. Not soldiers, understand. Farmers and smiths and hunters who can hold weapons. But they're willing."

"Two hundred and eight mages," Brynn said, doing the math. "Against thousands."

"Against an enemy that's predictable," Vera countered. "Shadow creatures fight in patterns.

They don't adapt, don't think creatively. Eight mages with a plan are worth a hundred warriors without one."

"And the fighters we're bringing are defending their homes," added one of the village leaders—a broad-shouldered woman named Marta. "They're not professional soldiers, but they're motivated. That counts for something."

Brynn sat down heavily, trying to process this. An actual army. Small, yes. Untrained, certainly. But real. People willing to fight beside her.

"Why?" she asked quietly. "Why are you all doing this? Most of you don't even know me."

"Because we know what happens if we don't," Vera said. "The Shadow Court has been growing for years. Slowly. Subtly. But we've felt it—reality getting thinner, boundaries weakening, strange things creeping through. If we don't stop them now, while they're still mostly sealed, we won't get another chance."

"And because you're trying," Marta added. "You could have run. Could have hidden. Instead you're fighting. That's worth supporting."

They spent the rest of the day planning. Vera spread out detailed maps of the Shadow Peaks and the surrounding terrain. Lucian's journal provided information about the Shadow King's forces and likely tactics.

"He'll know we're coming," Vera said. "The moment we enter the peaks, he'll sense us. So we can't rely on surprise."

"Then we rely on strategy," Thomas said. "We split our forces. Main army creates a distraction while a smaller group—Brynn, me, Kira, maybe two or three mages—slips past to reach the breach."

"The breach is in the central valley," Vera said, pointing to the map. "Called the Abyssal Vale. It's where reality is thinnest, where the Shadow Court's prison is most damaged. But getting there means fighting through the Shadow King's entire army."

"Unless we don't fight them," Kira said thoughtfully. "What if we go around? There are passes through the peaks that aren't on the main routes. Harder, more dangerous, but less guarded."

"Show me," Brynn said.

Kira traced a route on the map—narrow mountain paths that wound around the main valleys, approaching the Abyssal Vale from the south instead of the east. "It'll take longer. Three days instead of one. But if the Shadow King is expecting a frontal assault..."

"We hit him from behind while he's focused forward," Thomas finished. "I like it."

They refined the plan over hours of discussion. The main army would approach from the east, making as much noise as possible. When the Shadow King committed his forces to meet them, Brynn's team would enter from the south and race for the breach.

"The sealing takes twenty minutes," Brynn reminded them. "If the Shadow King realizes what we're doing and pulls forces back, we'll be overrun."

"Then the main army has to keep him convinced the real threat is in front of him," Vera said. "We make ourselves look more dangerous than we are. Illusion magic, showy displays, constant pressure. Make him think we're the primary assault."

"It's risky," Marta said. "The main army will take heavy casualties as a distraction."

"We all knew it was risky when we signed up," one of the other village leaders said quietly. "Better to die fighting than wait for the Shadow Court to consume us slowly."

The words hung heavy in the room.

"When do we move?" Vera asked.

Brynn touched the crown, feeling its pulse, sensing the three breaches. The Shadow Peaks breach was growing stronger by the day. In another month, it would open completely, and the Shadow King would emerge into the world with his full power.

"Two weeks," Brynn said. "That gives us time to gather all the fighters, practice working together, prepare supplies. And it gives me time to train with you," she looked at the mages, "to learn how to coordinate magic in battle."

Vera nodded. "Two weeks. We gather at Crossroads. From there, it's four days to the Shadow Peaks. Factor in time for the approach, and we're looking at three weeks until the final battle."

Three weeks. Twenty-one days to prepare for war.

It felt like both forever and not nearly enough time.

They dispersed that evening with assignments. Vera would coordinate the mages, teaching them to work in concert. Thomas would organize the fighters, teaching basic tactics and weapon drills. Kira would handle logistics—food, water, medical supplies, everything an army needed to function.

And Brynn... Brynn would train. With the mages to learn magical coordination. With Thomas to improve her sword work. With the crown to unlock whatever final knowledge it held about sealing breaches permanently.

Because the Abyssal Vale breach couldn't just be weakened. It had to be sealed permanently, or everything they'd done would be for nothing.

That night, alone in her room at the inn, Brynn pulled out Lucian's journal and turned to the final pages. Here, his handwriting grew shakier, the notes more desperate.

The permanent seal requires a sacrifice, he'd written. *Not of life, necessarily, but of power. The guardian must pour enough of themselves into the sealing that the breach cannot reopen. How much is enough? I don't know. Different guardians have given different amounts. Some survived. Some didn't.*

Lyra Stormblade gave everything. Used her own life force to create the prison and seal the Shadow Court. It bought a century of peace. But it killed her.

Will you have to do the same, future guardian? Or have you found another way? I hope you have. I hope my work helps you survive what Lyra could not.

Brynn closed the journal slowly. A sacrifice. Of course there would be a sacrifice. The crown had been preparing her for this from the beginning—showing her what it meant to be a guardian, what it cost.

She touched the crown gently. "Will I survive the permanent sealing?"

The crown's response was gentle but honest. *I don't know. It depends on how strong you've become. On how much of yourself you're willing to give. On whether the balance demands your life or merely your power.*

"And you won't tell me which it is?"

I can't. The choice must be yours, made freely, without knowing the outcome. That's what makes it a true sacrifice.

Brynn lay awake for hours, thinking about sacrifice and duty and whether she was ready to die at nineteen for a world that would never know her name.

She didn't know. But she knew she'd do it anyway if it came to that.

Because that's what guardians did.

The next two weeks blurred together in a haze of training and preparation. Brynn spent mornings with the mages, learning to coordinate her light-based power with their elemental magic. Fire and light combined into searing lances. Water and light created shields that could reflect shadow attacks. Earth and light made walls that corrupted creatures couldn't pass.

Afternoons were for weapon training. Thomas drilled her relentlessly, teaching her not to rely solely on the crown's power. "What happens if you're exhausted?" he'd ask, swinging at her with practice swords. "What if the crown has nothing left to give? You need steel and skill, not just magic."

Evenings were for logistics. She'd meet with Marta and the other village leaders, discussing supply lines and evacuation plans for if things went wrong. They were practical people who understood that war meant casualties.

"We're sending our people to die," Marta said bluntly one evening. "We all know it. Some of them won't come back. But if we don't try, none of us survive. So we do what we must."

The fighters arrived over those two weeks— small groups from a dozen villages, adding up to the promised two-fifty. They were farmers and hunters and merchants, not soldiers. But Vera's mages taught them basic shield formations. Thomas taught them to fight in lines, to support each other. And gradually, impossibly, they began to look like an army.

On the morning of the fifteenth day, Brynn stood on Crossroads' walls and watched the assembled forces below. Two hundred and fifty fighters, eight mages, dozens of support personnel managing supplies and medical care. And at the center, three people she trusted with her life— Thomas, Kira, and Vera.

"It's not much of an army," Vera said, joining her on the wall. "But it's what we have."

"It'll be enough," Brynn said, trying to believe it. "It has to be."

"You know you might die in the sealing," Vera said—not a question.

"Yes."

"And you're going anyway."

"Yes."

Vera studied her for a long moment. "Lucian chose wrong. The crown chose right. I see that now."

That afternoon, they marched east toward the Shadow Peaks. Two hundred and fifty fighters, eight mages, and one guardian wearing a crown that pulsed with barely contained power.

The war had begun.

Chapter 18: The March To War

The army moved slowly.

Brynn had expected that—farmers and merchants weren't trained soldiers, didn't know how to march in formation or maintain supply lines. But the reality was harder than she'd imagined. They covered barely fifteen miles the first day, half what she'd hoped for.

Thomas spent hours riding up and down the column, organizing stragglers, settling disputes, making sure no one fell too far behind. Kira managed the supply wagons with iron efficiency, rationing food and water to ensure they'd have enough for the return journey.

If there was a return journey.

On the second night, they made camp in a broad valley with good sight lines in all directions. Brynn stood guard duty even though she didn't have to, walking the perimeter and checking on the fighters.

Most were nervous. Some were terrified. A few looked eager, spoiling for a fight. Those worried Brynn most—the ones who didn't understand what they were walking into.

"Can't sleep?" Thomas asked, falling into step beside her.

"Not really. You?"

"Same." He was quiet for a moment. "Half of these people will die, won't they?"

Brynn wanted to lie, to reassure him. But he deserved honesty. "Probably more than half. The Shadow King has thousands of corrupted creatures. We have two-fifty fighters and eight mages. The math doesn't work in our favor."

"Then why are they coming? They have to know the odds."

"Because sometimes the right thing to do is also the suicidal thing to do," Brynn said. "And they're brave enough to do it anyway."

They walked in silence, listening to the camp settling down for the night. Somewhere, someone was singing—a bawdy drinking song that got laughs from the surrounding tents. Normal soldiers doing normal things before an abnormal battle.

"I'm scared," Thomas admitted quietly.

"Good," Brynn said. "Fear means you understand the stakes. It's the people who aren't scared I worry about."

"Are you scared?"

Brynn looked at him—this boy she'd grown up with, who'd followed her into danger without question, who'd stood by her through everything. "Terrified. Every moment. But I keep moving anyway."

Thomas took her hand, squeezed gently. "Whatever happens in the Shadow Peaks—"

"Don't," Brynn interrupted. "Don't make this a goodbye speech. We're both surviving this. Both of us. That's not negotiable."

Thomas smiled slightly. "Not negotiable. Right. I'll remember that when the Shadow King's armies are trying to kill us."

"You do that."

They completed the circuit of the camp and returned to the command tent where Vera and the other leaders were still awake, studying maps by candlelight.

"Problem," Vera said without preamble. "Scouts report shadow beasts in the hills ahead. Not many, maybe a dozen, but they're between us and the southern pass we wanted to use."

"Can we go around?" Brynn asked.

"Yes, but it adds two days to the journey. We'd hit the Shadow Peaks later than planned, giving the Shadow King more time to prepare."

"And if we fight through?"

"We lose people," Vera said bluntly. "In the dark, against shadow beasts, probably twenty or thirty casualties before we clear them. Maybe more if they're smart about it."

Brynn studied the map, thinking through options. Both choices were bad. Delay meant giving the enemy time to prepare. Fighting meant losing people before they even reached the real battle.

"We fight through," she decided. "Tomorrow morning, before dawn. I'll lead the attack with the mages. The fighters stay back until we've cleared the worst."

"You sure?" Thomas asked.

"No. But we can't afford the delay. Every day we wait is another day the breach grows stronger."

Vera nodded approvingly. "Good. Fast decision, no second-guessing. That's what armies need from commanders."

"I'm not a commander," Brynn protested. "I'm just—"

"You're the guardian," Marta interrupted. "You wear the crown. You give the orders. Whether you think of yourself as a commander or not, that's what you are now."

Brynn wanted to argue, but Marta was right. Somewhere along the journey from Thornhaven to here, she'd stopped being just Brynn Thornwick: and become something else. A symbol. A leader. A commander of forces who'd pledged to follow her.

The weight of that settled on her shoulders alongside the crown.

They broke camp before dawn, moving quietly through the darkness. Brynn took point with Vera and three other mages, leaving Thomas to lead the main force. Kira stayed with the supply wagons, protected in the center of the column.

The shadow beasts waited in a narrow pass between hills—exactly where Vera's scouts had reported. Brynn could see them through the crown's vision, darkness given form and malice. They knew the army was coming. They'd positioned themselves to cause maximum chaos.

"On my signal," Brynn whispered. The mages spread out, taking positions that would let them hit the beasts from multiple angles. "Three. Two. One. Now!"

Light exploded from Brynn's hands, bright as noon sun, flooding the pass. The shadow beasts shrieked and recoiled. Before they could recover, fire rained down from Vera's position, burning through shadow flesh. Ice spears from another mage. Stone walls rising to trap and crush.

The fight lasted less than five minutes. When it was over, fifteen shadow beasts lay dead or dying, melting into pools of darkness that steamed in the morning air.

And three of the fighters who'd rushed forward despite orders to stay back lay dead too, throats torn out by shadow claws before anyone could reach them.

Brynn knelt beside the bodies—two men and a woman, none older than twenty-five. She hadn't known their names. Hadn't had time to learn everyone in the army.

"First casualties," Vera said quietly. "Won't be the last."

"I know," Brynn said. "But I should know their names. If they're dying for me, I should at least know their names."

Marta appeared, having rushed forward when the fighting ended. She looked at the bodies and her face went hard. "Marcus Wheaton. His wife is pregnant. Elena Swift. Best hunter in her village. And James Potter. Sixteen years old, lied about his age to join."

"Sixteen," Brynn repeated, feeling sick.

"He wanted to protect his family," Marta said. "Wanted to be a hero. Now he's dead because he didn't follow orders and stay back."

"Now he's dead because I brought him here," Brynn said.

"No." Marta's voice was firm. "He's dead because the Shadow Court exists. Because the breaches are opening. Because something had to be done. You gave him a chance to do something meaningful with his life. That he died doing it... that's not your fault."

They buried the dead quickly—no time for elaborate funerals, but they carved the names into stones and placed them at the pass. Future travelers would know that people had died here fighting monsters.

The army moved on, quieter now, more sober. The reality of what they were marching toward had just become very real.

Two more days brought them to the foothills of the Shadow Peaks. The mountains rose before them like jagged teeth, dark stone that seemed to absorb light rather than reflect it. And hanging over everything was a pall of darkness that had nothing to do with weather.

"The breach is close," Brynn said, feeling it through the crown. "Maybe a day's march into the peaks."

"Then we split here," Vera said. "Main army continues east, making noise and drawing attention. Your team goes south, through the hidden passes."

They'd refined the plan over the march. The main force—two hundred fighters and five mages—would approach the Abyssal Vale from the east, engaging the Shadow King's army directly. Meanwhile, Brynn would lead a strike team of Thomas, Kira, Vera, and two other mages through southern passes that scouts had confirmed were lightly guarded.

The strike team would reach the breach while the Shadow King was distracted. Twenty minutes to seal it permanently. Then either retreat or, if the main army was being overwhelmed, try to help.

It was a desperate plan that required everything to go perfectly. But it was the only plan they had.

"Marta leads the main force," Brynn said. "She's got the most experience managing large groups. Vera, you coordinate the mages."

"What if we fail?" Marta asked bluntly. "What if the Shadow King breaks through us before you seal the breach?"

"Then you retreat," Brynn said. "Don't throw lives away in a lost cause. Get as many people out as you can."

"And leave you in there?" Thomas protested.

"If necessary, yes," Brynn said firmly. "The breach matters more than any of us. Even me. If we can't seal it, at least buy time for another guardian to try later."

The commanders nodded, but Thomas looked mutinous. Brynn made a mental note to talk to him privately before they split.

That night, the army made camp one last time as a unified force. Tomorrow, they'd separate—most heading east to war, a few heading south to what might be a suicide mission.

Brynn found Thomas sitting alone at the camp's edge, sharpening his sword with methodical precision.

"You're angry," she said, sitting beside him.

"I'm not leaving you," Thomas said. "Whatever orders you give, whatever you say about the greater good—I'm not leaving you to die alone in those mountains."

"I might not die."

"You read Lucian's journal. You know the permanent seal requires a sacrifice. You know you might have to give everything to close that breach." His hands shook slightly on the sword. "And you're going to do it anyway."

"I have to," Brynn said softly. "If I don't seal it permanently, everything we've done is temporary. The Shadow King will just break through again, and someone else will have to face this same choice."

"So we face it together," Thomas insisted. "That's what you've always said. We're in this together."

"And we are. You'll be there with me at the breach. You, Kira, Vera. I won't be alone."

"Until you have to make the sacrifice. Then you'll be alone in the only way that matters."

Brynn took his hands, stilling the shaking. "Thomas. Listen to me. I don't know if I'll survive the sealing. The crown won't tell me. But I know this—whether I survive or not, I need you to live. Someone has to carry on. Someone has to tell the story of what happened here. Someone has to make sure the sacrifices meant something."

"Don't ask me to be the one who survives while you die," Thomas said, his voice breaking.

"I'm not. I'm asking you to be strong enough to live with whatever happens. To not throw your life away in grief if I don't make it. To honor what we did by building something better in the after."

They sat in silence, holding hands, while around them the camp prepared for the last night before war.

"I love you," Thomas said finally. "I've loved you since we were children, and I'll love you until I die. I need you to know that."

"I know," Brynn said, tears streaming down her face. "I've always known. And I love you too. In every way that matters."

They stayed like that until the first light of dawn began to paint the eastern sky.

Then they stood, gathered their gear, and prepared to march to war.

The army split at sunrise. Marta led the main force east, banners flying, drums beating, making as much noise as possible. They were the distraction, the sacrifice, the brave souls who'd hold the Shadow King's attention while Brynn's team slipped past.

Brynn watched them march away and felt the weight of command settle heavier than ever. She'd sent two hundred people to almost certain death. The math was brutal—the Shadow King's thousands against their hundreds. They'd slow him, hurt him, but they wouldn't win.

They were buying time with blood.

"Come on," Vera said quietly. "They're doing their part. Now we do ours."

Brynn's team—six in total—turned south and entered the Shadow Peaks through passes so narrow they had to walk single-file. The peaks loomed above them, dark stone that seemed alive with malice. And ahead, somewhere in the mountains' heart, the Shadow King waited.

The final battle was coming.

And Brynn had no idea if she was strong enough to survive it.

Chapter 19: The Shadow Peaks

The southern pass was worse than the maps had indicated.

What scouts had described as a "narrow but navigable path" was actually a series of precarious ledges barely wide enough for one person, with sheer drops into darkness on one side and sharp rock walls on the other. One misstep would mean a fall that ended in death.

Brynn went first, the crown providing just enough light to see by without attracting attention. Behind her came Thomas, then Kira, then Vera and the two other mages—a water specialist named Jakob and an earth mage called Thorne.

They moved in silence, every footstep measured, every breath controlled. The Shadow Peaks felt wrong in ways that made Brynn's skin crawl. Not just dangerous but malevolent, as if the mountains themselves had been corrupted by the breach's proximity.

Around midday, Thorne held up a hand, signaling for them to stop. He pressed his palm against the rock wall and closed his eyes, his magic reaching into the stone.

"Something ahead," he said quietly. "Living things, but wrong. Moving in patterns. Patrolling."

"Shadow warriors?" Thomas asked.

"Or worse," Vera said. "The Shadow King wouldn't leave the southern approaches completely unguarded. He's smart enough to anticipate someone trying to flank him."

Brynn extended the crown's awareness, feeling past the immediate rock walls into the space beyond. And yes—she felt them now. Not shadow beasts, which were simple creatures driven by instinct. These were organized, intelligent, moving in coordinated patterns.

Shadow warriors. At least two dozen of them.

"Can we go around?" Kira asked.

"Not without adding hours to the journey," Thorne replied, his hand still against the rock. "And I'm not certain there is another route. This pass might be the only way through this section of the peaks."

"Then we fight through," Brynn said. "Fast and quiet. Kill them before they can raise an alarm."

"Six of us against two dozen of them," Jakob said nervously. "That's not good odds."

"It's better than it sounds," Vera countered. "Shadow warriors are strong but predictable. They fight in formation, follow patterns. We can use that."

They spent the next hour creeping forward until they had eyes on the enemy. The shadow warriors were exactly as Vera had described— humanoid figures made of solid darkness, armed with weapons that looked like crystallized shadow. They moved in precise patterns, clearly patrolling routes they'd walked a thousand times.

"There," Vera whispered, pointing to a narrow section of the pass where the patrol routes converged. "If we hit them there, we can funnel them, prevent them from surrounding us."

Brynn studied the terrain and nodded. "Jakob, can you create ice on the approach? Make it harder for them to maneuver?"

"Easily," Jakob confirmed.

"Thorne, block the rear exit. Stone walls, trap them in the killing zone."

"Done."

"Thomas, Kira, you're with me at the front. We hold the line while the mages do the real work." Brynn looked at each of them. "This needs to be fast. One of those warriors escapes, and they'll alert the

Shadow King. Then he'll know we're coming from the south."

"Fast and lethal," Vera agreed. "On your signal."

They positioned themselves silently, waiting for the next patrol rotation. When the shadow warriors entered the killing zone—twelve of them in two neat lines—Brynn gave the signal.

Jakob's ice flash-froze the ground beneath the warriors' feet. They slipped, stumbled, breaking formation. Before they could recover, Thorne's stone walls erupted from the ground, blocking both exits from the killing zone.

Trapped.

Brynn, Thomas, and Kira charged from the front while Vera unleashed fire from above. The shadow warriors recovered quickly, raising weapons to defend themselves, but the ambush had done its work. They were disorganized, unable to use their superior numbers effectively in the confined space.

Thomas's sword cut through shadow flesh, finding the cores of darkness that sustained the warriors. Kira's blade flashed in the dim light, seeking throats and hearts. And Brynn channeled the crown's power into concentrated beams of light that burned through shadow armor.

The fight lasted perhaps three minutes. When it was over, twelve shadow warriors lay dead or dying, dissolving into pools of darkness that steamed against Jakob's ice.

"The other twelve?" Thomas asked, breathing hard.

"Still on patrol," Thorne said, his hand against the rock again. "They haven't noticed anything wrong yet. We have maybe five minutes before they circle back and see what happened."

"Then we move," Brynn said. "Fast and quiet. Get past them before they realize we're here."

They ran, not caring about stealth anymore, just speed. Behind them, Brynn heard shouts of alarm as the remaining shadow warriors discovered their dead companions. But by then, Brynn's team had already put significant distance between them and the patrol.

They ran for an hour, following the pass as it wound deeper into the Shadow Peaks, until finally Vera called for a halt.

"We're clear," she said, gasping for breath. "They're not following. Either they don't know which way we went, or they're reporting back to the Shadow King instead of chasing."

"Reporting back is worse," Thomas said. "Now he knows someone's coming from the south."

"Maybe," Brynn said. "Or maybe he'll think it was just a scouting party. Either way, we have to assume he's alert now. No more ambushes. We move fast and hope we reach the breach before he can organize a proper defense."

They pushed on through the afternoon and into evening, stopping only briefly to eat cold rations and catch their breath. The pass opened up eventually into a series of interconnected valleys, and the going became easier even as the corruption grew more intense.

The sky above was permanently twilight, no sun visible despite it being hours until sunset should arrive. The air tasted like copper and ash. And in the distance, Brynn could hear sounds—not animal sounds, but the groans and crashes of something massive moving.

The Shadow King's armies on the march.

"They're engaging the main force," Vera said, hearing the same sounds. "Marta's attack has drawn them east."

"Then the distraction worked," Thomas said. "They're buying us time."

They're dying, Brynn thought but didn't say. Buying us time with blood.

Night fell—or what passed for night in the Shadow Peaks' eternal gloom. They made camp in a cave that Thorne checked carefully for structural stability. No fire—too risky. Just cold food and colder knowledge that tomorrow would bring the final confrontation.

Brynn couldn't sleep. She sat at the cave entrance, watching the darkness, feeling the breach pulsing somewhere ahead like a wound in reality.

Kira joined her quietly. "Nervous?"

"Terrified," Brynn admitted.

"Good. Me too." Kira was silent for a moment. "I never thanked you properly. For letting me come on this quest. For trusting me when I was just a random person you met by a river."

"You've more than earned that trust," Brynn said.

"Have I? I'm not a fighter. Not really. I can hold a sword, but I'm not skilled like Thomas. I'm not powerful like the mages. What am I contributing except another mouth to feed and another person for you to worry about?"

"You're the voice of reason when we lose our way," Brynn said. "The one who asks the questions no one else thinks to ask. The one who reminds us why we're doing this, not just how." She looked at Kira. "That matters more than you know."

Kira smiled slightly. "Sweet of you to say. But tomorrow, when we're fighting for our lives, I doubt philosophy will help much."

"Tomorrow, we each do what we do best," Brynn said. "You do yours. I'll do mine. Together, we'll be enough."

"You really believe that?"

"I have to," Brynn said simply. "Because if I don't believe we can win, we've already lost."

Dawn came gray and cold. They ate quickly, checked weapons and armor, and set out for what they hoped would be the final march.

The Abyssal Vale revealed itself gradually—first as a presence that made Brynn's crown pulse with recognition, then as a visible scar on the landscape. The valley was wrong in every way that mattered. The ground was cracked and bleeding darkness. The air shimmered with reality trying to hold itself together. And at the valley's center, a tear in space wider than any Brynn had seen before poured corruption into the world.

The breach.

And standing before it, waiting with the patience of something that had eternity to spend, was the Shadow King.

He was taller than the lieutenants had been—easily fifteen feet of darkness given form and purpose. His shape was vaguely humanoid but wrong in subtle ways—too many joints, limbs that bent at impossible angles, a head that seemed to see in all directions at once.

Around him stood an honor guard of shadow warriors—not dozens but hundreds, arrayed in perfect formation. And beyond them, Brynn could see the main army engaged with Marta's forces, a maelstrom of violence and chaos.

The Shadow King spoke, and his voice was the sound of stars dying:

"So. The infant guardian arrives at last. I've been watching your approach for hours. Wondering when you'd show yourself."

Brynn stepped forward, the crown blazing bright enough to push back the shadows around her. "You knew we were coming."

"Of course. Did you think yourselves clever with your splitting forces? Your distraction?" The Shadow King gestured dismissively. "I've been waging war for centuries. Your tactics are pedestrian at best."

"Then why let us approach?" Vera asked. "You could have sent your entire army south to crush us."

"Because I wanted to talk," the Shadow King said. "Before the inevitable slaughter. To offer you a choice."

"We're not interested in your offers," Thomas said, his sword raised.

"Aren't you?" The Shadow King leaned forward slightly, and Brynn felt the weight of his attention like a physical thing. "You've come to seal the breach. To trap my people back in their prison. But have you considered what we're offering?"

"Eternal stasis," Brynn said. "Everything frozen. No life, no growth, no change."

"No suffering," the Shadow King countered. "No pain, no betrayal, no death. We offer perfection. An end to the chaos that makes existence unbearable."

"An end to existence itself," Brynn said. "Life requires change. Growth requires struggle. You're not offering peace. You're offering oblivion dressed up pretty."

The Shadow King was silent for a moment. "You're young. You haven't lived long enough to be tired of living. But give it time. Give it decades of fighting, of losing people you love, of making impossible choices. Eventually, you'll understand. Eventually, you'll wish for the peace we offer."

"Maybe," Brynn said. "But not today. Today, I seal your breach and send you back to your prison."

"Then you'll do it over the bodies of everyone you brought with you," the Shadow King said. His voice grew harder. "Your distraction army is dying. Your small team stands against hundreds. You cannot reach the breach, let alone seal it. Surrender now. Accept the peace. Let the suffering end."

Brynn looked at her companions—Thomas, Kira, Vera, Jakob, Thorne. Five people she'd dragged into danger. Five lives depending on her decisions.

Then she looked at the Shadow King, at his honor guard, at the battle raging in the distance where good people were dying to buy her time.

"No," she said simply. "We don't surrender. We don't accept your 'peace.' We fight. And we win."

The Shadow King straightened to his full height. "Then you die. Honor guard—kill them all. But take the guardian alive. I want her to watch as we consume her world."

The shadow warriors charged.

And the final battle began.

Chapter 20: The Abyssal Vale

The shadow warriors moved as one—a wave of darkness and sharp weapons flowing toward Brynn's small team. Five hundred at least, maybe more, all converging on six defenders who were laughably outnumbered.

"Shield!" Vera shouted.

The three mages acted in concert. Vera's fire, Jakob's ice, and Thorne's stone combined into a barrier that blocked the first assault. Shadow weapons struck the shield and shattered, buying precious seconds.

"Thomas, Kira, protect the mages!" Brynn commanded. "They need to maintain the barrier!"

She channeled power through the crown, not into attacks but into enhancement. Light flowed from her into her companions, strengthening them, sharpening their reflexes, pushing human limits into something more.

Thomas's sword moved faster than should be possible, cutting through shadow warriors that made it past the barrier. Kira fought beside him, her blade finding gaps in shadow armor with deadly precision. Together, they held the flanks while the mages maintained the shield.

But it wasn't enough. There were too many enemies, and the shield was weakening under constant assault. Cracks appeared in the barrier, and shadow weapons began punching through.

"Brynn!" Vera shouted. "We can't hold this! We need to break through, reach the breach!"

Brynn assessed the situation in an instant. The breach was perhaps two hundred yards away, through the densest concentration of shadow warriors. A normal human couldn't make that run. But she wasn't entirely human anymore—not with the crown's power flowing through her.

"On my signal, drop the shield," Brynn said. "All three mages, give me everything you have. One massive attack to clear a path. Thomas, Kira, you're with me. We run for the breach. Mages, you hold here and keep the warriors busy."

"That's suicide," Jakob protested. "You'll be surrounded!"

"We're already surrounded," Brynn countered. "This way at least gives us a chance."

Vera met her eyes and nodded. "Make it count, guardian. Don't waste the opening."

"Now!" Brynn shouted.

The shield dropped. For one heartbeat, they were completely exposed. Then fire, ice, and stone erupted simultaneously, channeled and focused by three skilled mages working in perfect harmony.

A lance of elemental fury carved through the shadow warriors like a blade through water. Bodies dissolved, formations scattered, and for just a moment, a clear path opened to the breach.

Brynn ran.

She channeled the crown's power into her legs, into her body, pushing beyond human speed. Thomas and Kira followed, enhanced by the blessing she'd given them earlier. Behind them, she heard the shadow warriors reforming, heard Vera and the others fighting desperately to hold the enemy's attention.

They covered half the distance before the shadow warriors realized what was happening. A hundred voices shouted in alarm, and warriors began peeling away from the mages to intercept Brynn's run.

A shadow blade whistled toward her head. Thomas deflected it, never breaking stride. An arrow of darkness—Brynn hadn't known shadow warriors used ranged weapons—struck Kira's shoulder, but the woman pulled it out and kept running, her face set with determination.

One hundred yards to the breach. Fifty yards.

The Shadow King himself moved to intercept them, his massive form crossing the distance with impossible speed. He swung one massive arm, and darkness solid as steel crashed toward Brynn.

She ducked under it, rolled, came up still running. The breach was right there, so close she could feel its wrongness pulsing against her skin.

Twenty-five yards.

Thomas went down, a shadow warrior's blade finding his leg. He collapsed with a cry of pain but immediately threw his sword. The weapon spun through the air and embedded itself in the warrior who'd struck him, buying Kira time to drag him to his feet.

"Go!" Thomas shouted to Brynn. "We'll hold them! Seal it!"

Ten yards.

The Shadow King stood directly between Brynn and the breach, blocking her path. His eyes—if the darkness that passed for eyes could be called that—fixed on her with ancient malice.

"Clever," he said. "Clever enough to get this far. But no further."

Brynn didn't slow down. Instead, she channeled everything the crown had into a single burst of speed and light. She became a comet of pure radiance, too fast to track, too bright to look at directly.

She passed through the Shadow King's grasp, felt his fingers close on empty air, and then she was at the breach.

The sealing ritual required a circle of protection, materials, time. But Brynn had none of those things. The shadow warriors were already recovering, already moving to surround her. Thomas and Kira were fighting for their lives behind her, trying to reach her. The mages were too far away to help.

She had perhaps thirty seconds before she was overrun.

Not enough time for the ritual. Not even close.

The crown pulsed against her brow, and she felt it offering knowledge—a shortcut, a desperate measure, a way to seal the breach quickly but at terrible cost.

You can pour yourself directly into the sealing, the crown said. *Skip the ritual, use your own life force as the binding. It will seal the breach permanently. But the cost...*

"How much?" Brynn asked aloud.

Everything, the crown said simply. *All of your power, all of your life, everything you are. The breach will seal. The Shadow Court will be imprisoned forever. But you will be gone.*

Brynn looked back and saw Thomas fighting his way toward her, his leg bleeding, his sword moving in desperate arcs. Saw Kira beside him, her face set with determination despite her wounds. Saw Vera and the other mages holding off hundreds of enemies, buying time with their lives.

Saw all of them fighting because they believed in her. Believed she could stop this.

And she could. Just not the way they hoped.

"There has to be another way," Brynn said desperately. "Some other option."

There is, the crown said. *You could leave. Let the breach open fully. Let the Shadow Court emerge. Then maybe, decades from now, another guardian will arise who's strong enough to face them. That's the other option.*

"That's not an option," Brynn said.

Then you know what you must do.

The shadow warriors were closing in. The Shadow King was right behind them, his massive form blotting out what little light remained. In seconds, they'd reach her, and then everything would be lost.

"I'm sorry," Brynn whispered, not sure who she was apologizing to. Her friends. Her grandmother. Herself. "I'm sorry I'm not strong enough to find another way."

She placed both hands on the breach, feeling its corruption, its wrongness, its desperate desire to tear reality apart.

And she began to pour herself into it.

The crown's power flowed first—all the magic she'd accumulated, all the strength she'd gathered, draining out of her like water from a broken cup. The breach shuddered, began to close, but it wasn't enough.

Brynn gave more. Her memories, bright and terrible, flowing into the breach to fuel the sealing. She felt them leaving her—her grandmother's stories, Thomas's smile, Kira's laughter, Lucian's final words. All of it flowing away, becoming part of the seal.

The breach closed further, the edges beginning to knit together. But still not enough.

"Brynn!" Thomas's voice, distant now, fading. "What are you doing?!"

She couldn't answer. Couldn't spare the energy to speak. She gave more—her hopes, her dreams, the person she'd been and the person she'd hoped to become. All of it poured into the breach, fueling the seal, binding the Shadow Court back into their prison.

The breach was almost closed now. Just a little more.

Brynn felt herself diminishing. Not dying, exactly, but fading. Becoming less. The crown was quiet—it had given everything it could, and now only she remained.

One final push. One final sacrifice.

She gave everything she had left.

Her life force, her consciousness, her self—all of it poured into the breach in one last desperate surge of power.

The breach sealed with a sound like reality sighing in relief.

And Brynn fell into darkness.

The Shadow King watched the breach close and knew, with the certainty of centuries, that he'd lost.

The breach was sealed. Permanently. No amount of effort would break it from his side. The prison would hold now, perhaps forever, binding the

Shadow Court in their dimension while the world moved on without them.

He looked at the girl who'd done it—collapsed before the sealed breach, so still she might have been dead. The crown on her head still glowed faintly, but the light was guttering, fading, dying.

"She actually did it," the Shadow King said, almost in admiration. "She gave everything. Sacrificed herself completely."

The shadow warriors around him had stopped fighting, confused by their enemy's sudden collapse. Thomas and Kira had broken through to Brynn, were kneeling beside her, trying to wake her. The mages were rushing forward, abandoning their defensive position now that the breach was sealed.

"Kill them," the Shadow King said to his warriors. "Kill all of them. The breach may be sealed, but we're still here. We can still make them pay for what they've done."

The shadow warriors advanced, weapons raised.

And then light blazed across the battlefield.

Not from Brynn—she was unconscious, possibly dying. The light came from elsewhere, from the east, where the main army had been fighting.

Marta led the charge, what remained of the distraction force rallying for one final assault. They'd seen the breach seal, had seen Brynn fall, and they'd broken away from their own battle to come to her aid.

"For the guardian!" Marta shouted, her voice carrying across the Abyssal Vale. "For the girl who saved us all!"

Two hundred fighters—more than half dead, the survivors wounded and exhausted—crashed into the shadow warriors' flank. It shouldn't have been enough. The shadow warriors still outnumbered them, still had the Shadow King himself leading them.

But the shadow warriors weren't fighting anymore. Not really. With the breach sealed, they'd lost their connection to the Shadow Court, their source of power. They fought on but weakened with each passing moment, their forms becoming translucent, their blows losing strength.

The Shadow King felt it too—the prison reasserting itself, drawing him back toward the dimension where he belonged. He could fight it, could resist for a time, but eventually the pull would become irresistible.

He'd lost. The guardian had won.

"Fall back," he commanded his warriors. "There's nothing left here to fight for. The breach is sealed. The prison holds. Our time in this world is done."

The shadow warriors began to fade, dissolving like morning mist under sunlight. Within minutes, they were gone—returned to their prison, or perhaps simply ceasing to exist. The Shadow King couldn't tell anymore.

He looked one last time at Brynn, still lying motionless before the sealed breach.

"You were worthy," he said, though she couldn't hear him. "More worthy than any guardian in centuries. I hope the cost wasn't too high."

Then he too faded, returning to the prison, leaving the world behind.

Thomas cradled Brynn's head in his lap, tears streaming down his face. She wasn't breathing. Wasn't moving. The crown on her head barely glowed—just the faintest flicker, like an ember almost burned out.

"Don't you dare," he said, his voice breaking. "Don't you dare die. Not after everything. Not after we won. Please, Brynn. Please."

Kira was trying to find a pulse, her fingers pressed against Brynn's throat. "Nothing. I can't feel anything."

Vera pushed through the crowd that had gathered, the three mages right behind her. She placed her hands on Brynn's chest, channeling whatever power she had left into healing magic.

"She's alive," Vera said after a moment. "Barely. But alive. Everything that made her her... most of it's gone. She gave it to the sealing."

"Can you bring her back?" Thomas asked desperately.

"I don't know," Vera admitted. "I've never seen anything like this. She's not injured, exactly. She's... empty. Like someone poured out her soul to fill a cup."

"The crown," Jakob said suddenly. "Look at the crown. It's still glowing."

Everyone looked. The crown on Brynn's head pulsed weakly but steadily, like a heartbeat maintaining itself through will alone.

"It's keeping her alive," Thorne said. "Anchoring her somehow. As long as the crown exists, there's something left of her."

"Then we get her somewhere safe," Marta said, taking charge with the authority of someone used to crisis. "We get her medical attention, proper care, and we pray to whatever gods might be listening that she comes back to us."

They improvised a stretcher and began the long journey out of the Shadow Peaks. Behind them, the Abyssal Vale was already beginning to heal—the cracked ground mending, the poisoned air clearing, reality reasserting itself now that the breach was sealed.

The battle was over.

The war was won.

But their guardian lay unconscious, perhaps dying, and no one knew if she would ever wake up.

Chapter 21: The Long Sleep

Three days after the sealing, they reached Crossroads.

The town erupted when they saw the army returning—not in celebration but in grief. Two hundred and fifty fighters had marched east. Fewer than eighty came back. The casualties were worse than anyone had anticipated.

But they'd won. The breach was sealed. The Shadow Court was imprisoned. The world was safe.

For now.

They carried Brynn to the healer's guild, where the most skilled practitioners in the region gathered to examine her. The diagnosis was the same every time: she lived, but barely. Her body functioned, but the person inside it was gone or so deeply hidden that no magic could reach her.

"It's like she's sleeping," said Master Healer Cornelius, a man who'd treated everything from plague to demon possession. "But not ordinary sleep. This is deeper. Closer to death than life."

"How do we wake her?" Thomas asked. He'd barely left her side since they'd brought her back, sleeping in a chair beside her bed, eating only when forced.

"I don't know," Cornelius admitted. "This is beyond my knowledge. Beyond anyone's knowledge. She gave too much to the sealing. There might not be enough left to wake up."

The crown still rested on Brynn's head, refusing to be removed. Vera had tried once and found it would not budge—it was part of her now, fused somehow through the sealing process.

Days became weeks. The survivors of the battle dispersed, returning to their villages with stories of the brave girl who'd saved them all. Marta organized supplies for the wounded, coordinated care, made sure everyone who'd fought received what help could be given.

Kira stayed in Crossroads, translating between healers and gathering information from every source she could find about similar cases in history. There weren't many. Guardians who gave everything to seal breaches usually just died immediately. Lingering in this twilight state was unusual.

"I found one reference," Kira said two weeks after the battle, bringing an ancient tome to Thomas. "A guardian from three hundred years ago. She sealed a major breach and fell into what they called 'the long sleep.' She remained unconscious for five years. Then one day, she simply woke up. The text doesn't explain how or why."

"Five years," Thomas said hollowly.

"Or she might wake up tomorrow," Kira said. "The point is, there's precedent. People who gave everything to sealings have come back. It's possible."

Thomas clung to that hope like a drowning man to driftwood.

Vera visited regularly, though she spent most of her time organizing the surviving mages into a sort of early warning network. "The Shadow Court is sealed," she told Thomas during one visit, "but there are other threats. Other things that might break through. We need to be ready."

"Shouldn't the crown pass to someone else?" Thomas asked. "If Brynn's not waking up, shouldn't another guardian be chosen?"

"The crown chose her," Vera said, gesturing to the artifact that still glowed faintly on Brynn's head. "It hasn't released her yet. Until it does, she's still the guardian, conscious or not."

Thomas's father came to Crossroads, his leg still healing from the corruption-induced injury. He and Thomas had a long conversation—about regret, about the things they'd said while poisoned, about the son's choice to follow a girl on an impossible quest.

"I was wrong," his father said. "About everything. She was worth following. Worth believing in. And you were right to go with her."

"I'd do it again," Thomas said. "Every choice, every battle, every sacrifice. I'd make them all again."

His father smiled sadly. "I know. That's what makes you better than me."

A month after the battle, Father Benedict arrived from Thornhaven with news. "The village is healing. People are mending relationships, rebuilding trust. The corruption's effects are fading, though slowly." He looked at Brynn, lying so still in her bed. "How is she?"

"The same," Thomas said. "Always the same."

"The same is not dead," Father Benedict pointed out gently. "The same means there's still hope."

Hope became Thomas's anchor over the following months. Hope that Brynn would wake. That her eyes would open and she'd smile and everything would be all right again. He talked to her constantly, telling her about the day's events, about how people were rebuilding, about how the world she'd saved was getting better.

"You need to come back," he'd say. "We need you. I need you. Please, Brynn. Wake up."

The crown pulsed occasionally, responding to his voice or perhaps to something only it could sense. Vera suggested it was keeping Brynn alive, maintaining her body while her consciousness wandered somewhere else.

"Wandered where?" Thomas asked.

"Who knows? The space between dimensions. The realm of pure magic. Her own mind." Vera shrugged. "The crown is ancient, and its workings are mysteries. Trust it. If it's keeping her alive, there's a reason."

Six months after the battle, Thomas finally left Crossroads. Not permanently—he'd return every few days—but he needed to work, needed to do something besides wait. He took a job at the local smithy, forging tools and weapons, keeping his hands busy so his mind wouldn't spiral into despair.

Kira stayed, having nothing to return to. She'd found her purpose here, tending to Brynn and coordinating the network of information Vera was building. She'd also started writing—compiling the story of their quest, documenting everything from the map's discovery to the final battle.

"Someone should remember accurately," she said when Thomas found her working on the manuscript. "Someone should write down what actually happened, before the stories become legends and the legends become myths. Future guardians might need to know."

Eight months after the battle, something changed.

Brynn's eyes moved beneath their closed lids. Just a flicker, easily missed, but Thomas was watching and saw it immediately.

"She's dreaming," he said, calling for the healers. "She's actually dreaming."

Cornelius examined her and confirmed it. "Brain activity is increasing. Not waking yet, but closer. Something's happening inside her mind."

From that day forward, the signs multiplied. Small movements—fingers twitching, breath patterns changing, even once a soft sound that might have been a sigh. Brynn was coming back, slowly, incrementally, from wherever she'd been.

Thomas began reading to her from Kira's manuscript, figuring if anything would draw her back, it would be the story of what they'd accomplished. He read about the altar, about the Keeper, about their battles and sacrifices.

Ten months after the battle, on a morning that dawned clear and cold, Brynn's eyes opened.

Thomas was there, had been reading to her, and at first he didn't notice. Then he heard her voice —weak, rough from disuse, but hers:

"You're skipping parts."

Thomas dropped the manuscript, nearly knocked over his chair in his haste to reach her side. "Brynn? You're awake. You're actually awake."

She blinked slowly, focusing on him with effort. "How long?"

"Ten months. You've been asleep for ten months."

Brynn processed this, her expression unreadable. "The breach?"

"Sealed. Permanently. Just like you planned. The Shadow Court is imprisoned, probably forever. You saved us all."

Brynn tried to smile but managed only a weak grimace. "Then why do I feel like I lost something?"

"Because you gave everything to the sealing," Thomas said gently. "You poured yourself into it. The healers say most of what made you you is gone.

We thought..." His voice caught. "We thought you might never wake up."

"I didn't want to," Brynn admitted. "It was peaceful in the darkness. Easy. No weight, no responsibility, no burden. But I kept feeling the crown pulling at me, refusing to let me go. And I kept hearing your voice, reading those stories." She looked at him, really looked at him. "You stayed."

"Of course I stayed. Did you think I'd leave you?"

"You should have. Should have moved on, built a life. I gave you permission to let go."

"And I chose not to," Thomas said firmly. "I chose to wait. I chose to believe you'd come back. And you did."

Brynn's hand found his, squeezing weakly. "I remember... pieces. The breach opening. The Shadow King. Giving everything to the seal." She touched the crown with her free hand. "But there are gaps. Things missing. Like I can't quite remember who I was."

"Then we'll help you remember," Thomas promised. "However long it takes."

The next weeks were difficult. Brynn had to relearn how to walk, how to eat solid food, how to exist in her body again. Her memories returned slowly, inconsistently. She'd remember childhood clearly but forget yesterday. Recall the feeling of casting magic but not the name of the spell.

The crown remained constant—glowing softly, anchoring her, maintaining her existence when her own life force wasn't quite enough yet. Cornelius theorized it was slowly giving back what she'd poured into the sealing, rebuilding her piece by piece.

"You'll never be exactly who you were," he warned her. "The person who sealed that breach gave too much. But you're becoming someone new. Someone shaped by what you did."

Kira visited daily, bringing sections of the manuscript and reading them to Brynn. "Here's where you fought the first lieutenant. Remember? In the Corrupted Forest?"

Brynn would listen, and slowly the memories would surface. Not complete, not perfect, but there. Enough to know herself again, to remember what she'd fought for and why.

Three months after waking—a year since the battle—Brynn finally left the healer's hall. She walked through Crossroads on unsteady legs, Thomas supporting her when she stumbled, and for the first time she truly saw what she'd saved.

Children playing in the streets, untouched by corruption. Merchants trading without fear of shadow beasts. People living normal lives, unaware that they'd nearly lost everything.

"Was it worth it?" Thomas asked quietly as they sat in the town square, watching life flow around them. "Everything you gave?"

Brynn didn't answer immediately. She watched a little girl laughing as she chased a ball, watched her mother catch her and spin her around. Watched normal human joy and life and love.

"Yes," she said finally. "It was worth it."

Chapter 22: The Road Home

Spring came late to Thornhaven but arrived with the kind of vibrant intensity that made the long winter almost worthwhile. Trees that had looked dead for months suddenly exploded with green. Flowers that had been dormant for seasons bloomed overnight. And in her grandmother's garden, Brynn stood among the roses and tried to remember why this place had mattered so much.

Fifteen months since the sealing. Five months since waking. And she was still recovering.

"You're pushing too hard," Thomas said from the garden gate. He'd taken to following her everywhere—partly from affection, partly from worry that she'd collapse again.

"I'm fine," Brynn said automatically, though her legs trembled with exhaustion from the short walk from the cottage. "I just wanted to see the roses."

She'd come home to Thornhaven a month ago, once the healers agreed she was stable enough for travel. The village had welcomed her with a celebration that she'd barely been able to endure—

too many people, too much noise, too many faces she should remember but couldn't quite place.

Thomas's father had embraced her, tears streaming down his face. "You saved my son. Saved us all. How do we ever repay that?"

"You don't," Brynn had said simply. "You just live. That's payment enough."

Now she lived in her grandmother's cottage, surrounded by memories that felt more like stories than experiences. Kira had moved in to help—ostensibly as a caretaker but really as a friend who understood what Brynn was going through.

"The mages want to visit," Kira said that evening over dinner. "Vera sent word. She has questions about the crown, about what you remember from the sealing."

"Tell her to come," Brynn said. "I don't have many answers, but she's welcome to what I have."

Vera arrived two days later with Jakob and Thorne. They found Brynn in the garden—she spent most of her time there now, something about the growing things soothed her fractured mind.

"You look better," Vera said, settling onto the bench beside her. "Color in your cheeks. Not so skeletal."

"I'm eating more," Brynn confirmed. "Sleeping better. Kira says I'm almost human again."

"Almost?"

Brynn touched the crown, which had become such a part of her she barely noticed its weight anymore. "I'll never be fully human again. The sealing changed me. Made me something... else. I can feel it—the places where I gave pieces away and the crown filled the gaps. I'm part guardian, part crown, part whatever remained of who I used to be."

Vera nodded slowly. "The crown is keeping you alive. We've determined that much. Without it, you'd fade away—not enough life force left to sustain yourself."

"So I'm bound to it forever," Brynn said. "Can't remove it. Can't pass it on. Can't die as long as it exists."

"That bothers you?"

"Shouldn't it? I'm twenty years old, and I've already lived more than most people experience in eighty years. The idea of living centuries like this..." She gestured vaguely. "It's exhausting."

"Then rest," Vera said practically. "You sealed the major breach. The Shadow Court is imprisoned. There are no immediate threats that require a guardian's attention. So rest. Recover. Live quietly for a few years."

"Is that allowed? Can guardians just... stop?"

"You're the guardian," Vera pointed out. "You make the rules. If you want to spend the next decade baking bread in Thornhaven, who's to stop you?"

The idea was absurdly appealing. Brynn imagined it—quiet days in the garden, baking bread, talking with neighbors, living the simple life she'd left behind when she found the map in her grandmother's attic.

"What about the minor breaches?" she asked. "The crown says there are dozens scattered throughout the region. Small ones that don't threaten reality but still leak corruption."

"We're handling them," Jakob said. "Vera's organized the mages into teams. We seal the minor breaches as we find them. It's not permanent like your sealing, but it holds them closed for years at a time."

"And if something bigger appears?"

"Then we send for you," Thorne said. "But Brynn, that could be decades. Lyra Stormblade's sealing held for a century before it began to fail. Yours might hold even longer—you gave more to it than she did."

Brynn wasn't sure how to feel about that. Pride at doing better than the legendary guardian? Horror at what that success had cost? Both felt true.

The mages stayed for three days, sharing information about the network they'd built and the state of the region. The world was healing slowly. Villages corrupted by the breaches were recovering. People who'd been twisted by shadow influence were coming back to themselves. It would take years—decades maybe—but normalcy was returning.

"You should be proud," Vera said before leaving. "You did what needed doing. Made the hard choices. And you survived it, which is more than most guardians manage."

"It doesn't feel like survival," Brynn admitted. "It feels like I died and someone else woke up wearing my body."

"Give it time," Vera advised. "You're still recovering. The person you're becoming hasn't fully formed yet. But she will. And when she does, I think you'll be surprised at who you find."

After the mages left, Brynn spent long hours in her grandmother's study, reading through journals she'd left behind. Aubre had documented her own journey to the altar, her decision to walk away, her years of waiting and wondering if she'd made the right choice.

I saw you in the vision, Aubre had written. *Saw you standing where I stood, ready for what I couldn't face. And I knew my path was different. Not to claim the crown but to prepare the one who would.*

I hope I did right by you, granddaughter. I hope my stories and lessons were enough. I hope you forgive me for the burden I helped place on your shoulders.

Brynn traced the words with her finger, and for the first time since waking, she cried—not from grief but from understanding. Her grandmother hadn't abandoned her calling. She'd fulfilled it differently, by preparing the next guardian instead of being one herself.

"I forgive you," Brynn whispered to the empty room. "And thank you. For everything."

Summer arrived, hot and lush. Brynn's strength returned slowly but steadily. She could walk through the village without exhaustion now. Could help with harvest preparations, bake bread, do normal things without collapsing.

Thomas courted her properly, the way he'd never had time to before. Evening walks through the countryside. Picnics by the stream. Conversations that lasted until dawn about everything and nothing.

"What do you want?" he asked one evening as they sat by the water, watching fireflies dance in the twilight. "For the future. For your life. What do you actually want?"

Brynn considered the question carefully. Six months ago, she couldn't have answered it—couldn't have imagined wanting anything beyond survival. But now...

"Peace," she said finally. "For a while at least. Time to figure out who I am when I'm not fighting or dying or saving the world. Time to just... be."

"And after that?"

"I don't know. The crown says there will always be threats, always be work for guardians. But maybe not for years. Maybe not for decades. So maybe I have time to be human before I have to be a guardian again."

"And what does being human look like?"

Brynn looked at him—this boy she'd loved since childhood, who'd followed her into hell and helped drag her back out. "It looks like this. You, me, fireflies, and time to enjoy them. That's enough."

Thomas kissed her then, gentle and sweet, and Brynn felt something settle in her chest. Not healing exactly—she'd never fully heal from what she'd given to the sealing. But peace. Acceptance. The beginning of moving forward.

That fall, Thomas asked her to marry him. They were in the garden—where else?—surrounded by roses that Aubre had planted decades ago.

"I know it's fast," he said, kneeling among the flowers. "I know you're still recovering. But I've loved you my whole life, Brynn Thornwick:. I followed you to the end of the world and watched you save it. Now I want to follow you into whatever comes next. Will you have me?"

Brynn looked at the ring he offered—simple silver with a small red stone that matched the crown's color. She thought about duty and destiny and the burden of being a guardian. Thought about the centuries she might have to live, the battles yet to come, the sacrifices still waiting.

Then she thought about joy and love and the fact that she'd earned a little happiness after everything she'd given.

"Yes," she said, pulling him up to kiss him. "Yes, absolutely yes."

They married that winter in a small ceremony at the church. Father Benedict officiated, beaming with joy. Kira stood as Brynn's witness, having become the sister she'd never had. Thomas's father gave them his blessing and a house—the small cottage behind the forge where Thomas had grown up.

"Start your life there," his father said. "Build something good. You've earned it."

They did build something good. Not grand or legendary, just normal and human and theirs. Thomas worked at the forge. Brynn helped where she could, though she couldn't manage the physical labor yet. They hosted dinners for friends. They laughed and argued and made up. They were, for the first time in their lives, simply happy.

The crown never came off, and Brynn never forgot what she was. But for those months, she got to pretend she was just a girl married to a boy she loved, living in a village where the most exciting event was the summer festival.

It was, she thought, the best gift anyone could have given her.

Chapter 23: The Call

Two years after the sealing, on a morning that started like any other, Brynn woke to find the crown burning.

Not with heat—it never hurt her—but with urgency. Power pulsing against her brow, demanding attention, insisting something was wrong.

She sat up carefully, trying not to wake Thomas, and reached inward toward the crown's awareness.

A breach, the crown said immediately. *Not major, but growing. North, perhaps fifty miles. It's been opening slowly for weeks, and now it's reached critical mass.*

"Can the mages handle it?" Brynn asked silently.

Perhaps. But it would be safer if you went. Your permanent sealing is stronger than anything they can manage.

Brynn looked at Thomas, still sleeping peacefully. They'd had two years of peace. Two years of normal life. She'd been happy.

But she'd also known this moment would come. Known that being a guardian meant answering when the crown called, no matter how much she wanted to stay home.

She dressed quietly, packed a small bag, and left a note for Thomas: *Breach north. Back in a few days. Love you.*

Then she walked out into the pre-dawn darkness and began the journey north.

The breach was exactly where the crown indicated—in a forest that had gone strange, trees growing in spiral patterns, animals with too many eyes watching her from the shadows. Not as bad as the Corrupted Forest had been, but getting there.

Brynn found the breach easily—her power recognized it instantly. The tear was smaller than the ones she'd faced before, but left unchecked it would grow.

She didn't need the full ritual anymore. Two years of living with the crown had taught her shortcuts, ways to channel power more efficiently. She drew a quick circle, channeled her power through the crown, and sealed the breach in under five minutes.

Easy. Almost disappointingly so compared to the desperate battles she'd fought before.

But as she turned to leave, she felt something else—another breach, smaller, farther away. And beyond that, another. And another.

The crown showed her what she'd refused to see during her two years of peace: the world was still damaged from the Shadow Court's attempts to break through. Minor breaches were opening everywhere, dozens at a time, requiring constant attention to keep sealed.

"This is what guardian work actually looks like," Brynn said aloud. "Not grand battles. Just constant maintenance. Endless small fights to hold back the darkness."

Yes, the crown confirmed. *This is the burden. Not dramatic, not legendary, just necessary.*

Brynn sealed the second breach, then the third. It took her a week to return home, and by then she'd sealed eight minor breaches. Thomas met her at the door, relief and concern warring on his face.

"I was worried," he said, pulling her into his arms. "Your note didn't say how long you'd be gone."

"I didn't know," Brynn said honestly. "One breach became eight. And the crown says there are more. Dozens more. All over the region."

"Then we deal with them," Thomas said simply. "Together. Like always."

"Thomas, you have work. The forge. Your life here."

"My life is with you," he corrected. "If being with you means traveling to seal breaches, then that's what we do. Besides—" he smiled slightly, "—normal was getting boring anyway."

They fell into a pattern over the following months. Brynn would sense a breach through the crown. She and Thomas would travel to it, seal it, return home. Sometimes the journey took days. Sometimes weeks. But they always returned to Thornhaven, to the small cottage behind the forge, to the life they'd built.

Kira often joined them, her translation skills proving useful when they traveled to regions where other languages were spoken. She'd become a sort of guardian's chronicler, documenting each breach sealed, each danger averted. "Future guardians will need to know," she said. "Need to understand what the work actually involves."

Three years after the sealing, Vera sent word that she'd organized the mages into a formal Guild. They'd taken responsibility for the smaller breaches, leaving only the most dangerous for Brynn. "You don't have to save the world every week," Vera's letter said. "Learn to delegate."

Brynn tried. But there were some breaches only she could seal permanently, and knowing that people were relying on temporary solutions when permanent ones were possible bothered her more than she wanted to admit.

Four years after the sealing, Thomas and Brynn's first child was born—a daughter they named Aubre, after Brynn's great grandmother. The crown pulsed with warmth when Brynn held her baby, and she felt the weight of new responsibility settling alongside the old.

"What if there's a breach while I'm nursing her?" Brynn asked Thomas, only half-joking. "What if something happens and I have to choose between being a mother and being a guardian?"

"Then we figure it out," Thomas said. "Same as we figure out everything else. Together."

Aubre grew quickly, bright and curious and utterly unafraid of the crown her mother wore. She'd reach for it with chubby baby hands, laughing when it glowed in response to her touch. "She's got magic," Vera observed during one visit. "Not much yet, but it's there. Your daughter might be the first child born to an active guardian in centuries."

"Will she have to be a guardian too?" Brynn asked, fear clutching her heart.

"Not necessarily. The crown chooses. But having guardian blood might make her a candidate when she's older." Vera paused. "How do you feel about that?"

Brynn looked at Aubre, sleeping peacefully in her father's arms. "I hope she never has to make the choices I made. Never has to give what I gave. But if the crown calls her..." She touched the artifact on her head. "Then I'll prepare her the way my grandmother prepared me. And I'll trust she'll be ready."

Five years after the sealing, on the anniversary of that desperate day in the Abyssal Vale, Brynn made a pilgrimage to the Shadow Peaks.

Thomas and Kira came with her, along with Marta and a few others who'd survived the final battle. They stood at the edge of the Abyssal Vale—now green and growing, all signs of corruption gone—and remembered.

"Two hundred and fifty went to war," Marta said quietly. "Eighty came back. Those numbers still hurt."

"They always will," Brynn agreed. "But look what they bought. The world is healing. The breaches are manageable. The Shadow Court is sealed. Those one hundred and seventy people gave their lives for this. For peace."

They placed a marker—a simple stone carved with the names of everyone who'd died in the battle. Future travelers would know what had happened here. Would understand the cost of the peace they enjoyed.

As they turned to leave, Brynn paused, sensing something. Not a threat exactly, but a presence. She reached out with the crown's awareness and felt... watching. Something or someone, observing from beyond the veil of reality.

The Shadow King? No, he was sealed away. But his attention, perhaps. His acknowledgment that the guardian who'd defeated him was still alive, still vigilant, still ready to fight if necessary.

We're still here, Brynn thought toward that presence. *Still watching. You're not getting out.*

The presence faded, and Brynn smiled grimly. Good. Let the Shadow Court know their prison held. Let them know the guardian who'd sealed them wasn't going anywhere.

They returned to Thornhaven as summer turned to fall. Aubre was learning to walk, stumbling around the cottage with determination that reminded Brynn painfully of herself at that age.

Thomas's forge was thriving, his reputation for quality work spreading throughout the region.

And Brynn continued her guardian work—sealing breaches, fighting corruption, maintaining the balance. Not grand battles anymore, just steady work. The kind that didn't make legends but kept the world safe.

"Is this enough?" Thomas asked one evening as they sat in the garden, Aubre playing at their feet. "This life we've built. Is it what you wanted?"

Brynn considered the question. Five years ago, she'd been dying in the Abyssal Vale, giving everything to seal a breach. Three years ago, she'd been barely alive, recovering in a healer's hall. Now she was a wife, a mother, a guardian who'd found a way to balance duty with life.

"It's more than I dared hope for," she said honestly. "More than I thought possible. So yes. This is enough."

Aubre looked up at her mother's voice and smiled—that pure, uncomplicated joy of a child who knows nothing of sacrifice or duty or the weight of saving the world.

"More than enough," Brynn amended, picking up her daughter. "This is everything."

Chapter 24: The Shadow Stirs

Ten years after the sealing, Brynn woke from a nightmare that wasn't really a nightmare at all.

She'd dreamed of the Shadow Court—not attacking, not breaking free, just existing in their prison. Waiting with the patience of beings who'd been imprisoned for a century already and could wait a century more. Watching the world through cracks in reality that were too small to pass through but large enough to see.

And they were learning.

Brynn sat up carefully, trying not to wake Thomas or Aubre, who'd crawled into their bed sometime during the night. The crown pulsed against her brow, confirming what the dream had shown her.

The Shadow Court was adapting. Not breaking out—they couldn't, not after the permanent seal. But adapting to their prison, finding ways to influence the world despite the barriers that held them.

"How?" Brynn whispered to the crown.

Through dreamers, the crown replied. *Those with natural sensitivity to magic. The Shadow Court speaks to them in sleep, plants ideas, subtly corrupts without ever manifesting physically.*

"Can they break the seal that way?"

No. But they can prepare the ground for the next guardian's failure. Plant doubts, create chaos, weaken society until resisting them seems impossible.

Brynn got up and went to the study—the small room where she'd moved her grandmother's books and papers after the wedding. She pulled out Lucian's journal, which she kept in a locked drawer, and flipped to a section she'd marked years ago.

The Shadow Court is patient, Lucian had written. *They think in centuries, not years. One defeat doesn't end them. They simply adjust their strategy and try again. Guardians who think they've won permanently are the ones most vulnerable to the next attack.*

Brynn had understood that intellectually. But she'd hoped—foolishly, perhaps—that her sacrifice had bought more time. That she could live out her life in peace, raise her daughter, grow old beside Thomas without having to fight again.

Instead, the fight was just changing forms.

She spent the next weeks researching, consulting with Vera and the Mage's Guild, trying to understand the scope of the problem. And it was bigger than she'd feared.

All across the region, people were having strange dreams. Not nightmares exactly, but unsettling visions of peace through surrender, of the futility of resistance, of how much easier life would be if they just accepted the inevitable.

"It's subtle," Vera reported during one of her visits. "Most people don't even realize they're being influenced. They just find themselves more cynical, more willing to accept that nothing can change, more likely to counsel against resistance when threats appear."

"The Shadow Court is preparing the next generation," Brynn said. "Making sure that when the seal weakens—and it will, eventually—there won't be anyone willing or able to fight them."

"Can we counter it?"

"We have to. But how do you fight whispers in dreams? How do you battle ideas without becoming the tyrants who suppress free thought?"

It was Kira who suggested the solution. "We tell stories. True stories. About what the Shadow Court actually is, what they actually offer. Give people the truth to weigh against the whispers."

So Brynn authorized Kira to publish her chronicle—the full, uncensored account of the quest, the battles, the sacrifices. The story of how the Shadow Court had been defeated not through grand heroics alone but through ordinary people choosing to resist impossible odds.

The chronicle spread throughout the region, copied and distributed by the Mage's Guild. And slowly, the whispers' influence began to fade. People who'd read the true account were better able to resist the dream-corrupts, to recognize the Shadow Court's promises for the lies they were.

But it wasn't enough. The Shadow Court adapted again, targeting children too young to read, planting fear instead of cynicism. Aubre, now ten years old, began having nightmares—not normal childhood fears but visions of shadow and corruption that left her screaming.

"Make it stop," she begged her mother after one particularly bad night. "Please, make the darkness stop talking to me."

Brynn held her daughter, channeling the crown's power to create a protective barrier around Aubre's mind. It worked temporarily, but maintaining it constantly was exhausting.

"This is what they want," Thomas said one night after Aubre had finally fallen into peaceful sleep. "They want to drain you, to keep you constantly defending, never resting. They're wearing you down."

"I know," Brynn admitted. "But what choice do I have? Let them corrupt my daughter?"

"No. But we need a better solution than you maintaining shields for every child in the region. That's not sustainable."

Vera proposed a ritual—a large-scale protection that would shield dreamers from the Shadow Court's influence. But it would require dozens of mages working in concert, and even then it would only last a few years before needing renewal.

"It's the best we can do," Vera said. "Unless you have a better idea."

Brynn didn't. So they performed the ritual—a massive undertaking that involved mages from across the region gathering at the sealed breach in the Abyssal Vale. Brynn anchored the spell, channeling the crown's power to make it as strong as possible, while the other mages fed their own magic into it.

When it was complete, a barrier settled across the region like an invisible dome. Dreamers slept peacefully again. The Shadow Court's whispers couldn't penetrate.

"For now," Vera cautioned. "This will hold for maybe five years. Maybe ten if we're lucky. Then we'll need to do it again."

"Then we do it again," Brynn said. "As many times as necessary. For as long as I'm alive, the Shadow Court doesn't get to corrupt our children."

The next years fell into a new pattern. Guardian work wasn't just sealing breaches anymore —it was maintaining barriers, teaching young mages to recognize corruption, counseling leaders on how to keep their communities resilient against subtle influence.

Aubre grew into adolescence, bright and strong and increasingly aware of her mother's burden. "Will I have to be a guardian too?" she asked on her fourteenth birthday. "Will the crown choose me when you're gone?"

"I don't know," Brynn answered honestly. "The crown chooses who it chooses. But Aubre—" she took her daughter's hands, "—if it does choose you, you don't have to accept. You can walk away. Live a normal life. I'd never blame you for that."

"Did Grandmother give you that choice?"

"In a way. She prepared me, but she never forced me. When the time came, the choice was mine."

Aubre nodded thoughtfully. "If the crown calls me, I think I'd answer. Not because I have to, but because..." She struggled for words. "Because if I can help, how can I not?"

Brynn heard her own words from years ago echoed back, and felt pride and fear in equal measure. Her daughter had inherited more than magic—she'd inherited the sense of duty that made guardians of ordinary people.

Fifteen years after the sealing, on a morning that felt like any other, Brynn felt something shift.

The barrier protecting dreamers wavered. Not breaking, not yet, but weakening faster than predicted. The Shadow Court was pushing against it, testing it, learning its structure so they could undermine it more effectively next time.

"They're adapting again," Vera said when Brynn reported the problem. "Finding weaknesses in our defenses. It's like fighting an enemy that learns from every defeat."

"Because they are learning," Brynn said. "The Shadow Court isn't mindless. They're intelligent, patient, and they have literally nothing to do but study our defenses and figure out how to counter them."

"So what do we do?"

"We adapt too. Change our defenses, keep them guessing, never let them completely understand our capabilities." Brynn paused. "And we start training a new generation. Not just of mages, but of people who understand what we're facing and why it matters. Build resilience into the culture itself."

It was ambitious. Maybe impossible. But it was also necessary.

Brynn began traveling more, speaking at villages and towns, teaching about the Shadow Court and why resistance mattered. She showed people the scars from her battles, told them honestly about the costs. But she also showed them that victory was possible. That ordinary people could stand against impossible odds and win.

Slowly, a new generation grew up understanding what was at stake. Young mages joined the Guild specifically to help maintain the barriers. Village leaders coordinated defense plans. Hunters and soldiers trained for the day when shadow beasts might return.

They were building something that transcended Brynn—a societal commitment to resist corruption, to maintain the balance, to never let the Shadow Court win.

"This is your real legacy," Kira said one evening as they sat reviewing the network they'd built. "Not the dramatic sealing, but this. A whole region that understands why guardians matter and actively supports them."

"I just hope it's enough," Brynn said.

"It will be," Kira assured her. "Because even after you're gone, it will continue. That's what makes it powerful."

After you're gone. The words hung in the air, heavy with implication.

Brynn was twenty-nine now. Thanks to the crown, she'd aged slowly—looked younger than her years, would probably live much longer than normal humans. But she wasn't immortal. Eventually, she would die. And then what?

The crown would choose another guardian. Someone from the next generation. Maybe Aubre, maybe someone else. And that person would inherit not just the crown but everything Brynn had built—the network, the knowledge, the society prepared to resist.

"I need to write it all down," Brynn said suddenly. "Everything I've learned about being a guardian. The practical stuff that's not in Lucian's journal or grandmother's notes. How to actually do this job day after day for decades."

"I'll help," Kira offered. "We'll make it comprehensive. A guardian's manual, essentially."

They spent the next year on the project, documenting everything from how to sense breaches to how to maintain barriers to how to build community support for guardian work. It became a thick volume, added to the collection in the study—Lucian's journal, Aubre's writings, and now Brynn's manual.

"Future guardians will have a complete library," Thomas observed, looking at the accumulated wisdom. "More knowledge than any guardian in history."

"They'll need it," Brynn said. "The Shadow Court gets smarter with each generation. Future guardians will face challenges we can't imagine."

That night, lying beside Thomas with Aubre asleep down the hall, Brynn felt the crown pulse with something that might have been satisfaction.

You're doing well, it said. *Building something that will outlast you. That's what guardians should do.*

"Will it be enough?" Brynn asked. "When I'm gone, when the next guardian takes over, will what I've built be enough to keep the Shadow Court sealed?"

I don't know, the crown admitted. *But you're giving them the best chance possible. That's all any guardian can do.*

Brynn closed her eyes, letting that truth settle. She'd saved the world once through dramatic sacrifice. Now she was saving it through slow, patient building. Both were necessary. Both were the guardian's burden.

And she'd carry it until she couldn't anymore. Then she'd pass it on, trusting that the next guardian would be ready.

Because that's what guardians did.

Chapter 25: The Guardian's Legacy

Twenty-five years after the sealing.

Brynn stood in her garden—planted with cuttings from her grandmother's roses years ago—and felt the crown settle more heavily than usual. Not painfully, but noticeably. A reminder that even magical artifacts had limits.

"You're failing," she said to it quietly. "Aren't you?"

Not failing, the crown corrected. *Adjusting. I've kept you alive for a quarter century beyond what should have been possible. But the energy I poured into the sealing is finally depleting. Soon, I won't have enough power to maintain both the seal and you.*

"How long?"

Years. Maybe decades. But eventually, you'll have to choose—let the seal weaken to preserve your life, or maintain the seal and accept the consequences.

"That's not a choice," Brynn said. "The seal matters more than I do."

I know. That's why I chose you.

Brynn was forty-four now, though she looked younger thanks to the crown's influence. Aubre was twenty-five, a skilled mage in her own right and increasingly involved in guardian work despite never being formally chosen by the crown. Thomas had grayed gracefully, his hands still steady at the forge but his body showing the wear of decades of hard work.

They'd had a good life. Better than Brynn had any right to hope for after what she'd given to the sealing.

But everything ended eventually.

"I need to prepare Aubre," Brynn said aloud. "Need to make sure she's ready if the crown chooses her when I'm gone."

Aubre found her mother in the garden that evening. "You look thoughtful. Something wrong?"

"The crown is running out of power," Brynn said directly. "Eventually, it won't be able to keep me alive and maintain the seal simultaneously. When that happens, I'm going to choose the seal."

"Mother—" Aubre started, but Brynn held up a hand.

"I've known this was coming since I woke up all those years ago." The healers warned me I was living on borrowed time. Every year since has been a gift." She took her daughter's hands. "I'm not afraid of dying. I'm just afraid of leaving you unprepared if the crown chooses you next."

"What if it doesn't choose me?" Aubre asked. "What if I'm not worthy?"

"Then it will choose someone else, and you'll help them the way Kira and Thomas and Vera helped me. Either way, you're ready for what comes next."

They spent that evening in the study, going through all the accumulated knowledge—Lucian's journal, Aubre's writings, Brynn's manual, and other texts gathered over the years. Aubre had read it all before, but now they reviewed it with the understanding that this was no longer theoretical. Soon, this would be her responsibility.

"The barrier protecting dreamers needs renewal every eight years," Brynn explained. "It's scheduled for next spring. The regional breach network—Vera's got most of it covered, but these three locations—" she pointed at a map, "—tend to develop new tears. Someone needs to check them quarterly."

"I know all this," Aubre said gently. "You've been teaching me for years."

"I know. But there's a difference between knowing and doing. And I need to make sure—"

Brynn's voice caught. "I need to make sure you'll be okay when I'm not here to help."

"I won't be okay," Aubre said honestly. "Losing you will break something in me that might never fully heal. But I'll keep going. Because that's what you taught me. That guardians keep going even when they're broken."

That winter, Brynn began saying her goodbyes. Not dramatically—she wasn't dying immediately. But acknowledging that her time was limited, that she needed to make peace with the people and places that had mattered.

She visited Vera, now elderly herself but still sharp. "You built something good," Vera said. "The Mage's Guild is strong. The dream barriers hold. The breach network functions. You've set up every future guardian for success."

"I hope so," Brynn said.

"Don't hope. Know. I've lived a long time, watched a lot of people try to change the world. Most fail because they try to do everything themselves. You succeeded because you built a system that doesn't depend on you being alive. That's rare. That's valuable."

Brynn visited Marta, who'd retired from leadership but still kept tabs on the regional defense network. "The villages are prepared," Marta reported. "They know what to watch for, how to respond if corruption appears. You've given them the tools they need."

She visited the Abyssal Vale one last time, standing at the sealed breach and reaching out with the crown's awareness. The seal held strong—stronger than Lyra Stormblade's century-old seal had been at this point. Brynn's sacrifice had been even greater, and the result was even more permanent.

The Shadow Court can't break this, the crown confirmed. *Not from their side. Only if a future guardian deliberately unseals it could they escape. You've won, Brynn. Truly won.*

"For now," Brynn said. "Until the next threat, the next breach, the next battle."

That's all any victory ever is, the crown said. *Temporary. Giving the next generation a chance to face their own challenges. You've given them that chance. That's all anyone can do.*

Spring came again—the twenty-eighth since Brynn had found the map in her grandmother's attic. She was forty-six now and she could feel the crown's power dimming further. Not failing yet, but noticeably weaker than it had been.

Aubre noticed too. "Mother, you're fading. I can see it. The light in you is dimming."

"I know," Brynn said. "But the seal is holding. That's what matters."

They performed the dream barrier renewal that spring with Aubre taking a leading role. Brynn anchored the spell as always, but she could feel her daughter's power growing stronger, more confident. Ready to take over.

"The crown is preparing her," Brynn realized. "Getting her ready for when it has to choose a new guardian."

Summer brought visitors—Thomas's father, now very old, come to say goodbye to the granddaughter-in-law who'd saved his son's life. Kira, whose chronicles had made her famous throughout the region. Thorne and Jakob, still maintaining the breach network they'd helped establish.

"You look tired," Thomas said one evening after the visitors had left. They sat in the garden, watching fireflies dance as they had all those years ago when he'd first asked what she wanted.

"I am tired," Brynn admitted. "Ready to rest. But not yet. Not until I'm certain everything's in order."

"Everything is in order," Thomas said firmly. "You've prepared Aubre. You've built networks and systems. You've done everything possible. It's okay to let go."

"Is it though?" Brynn asked. "There's always more to do. More breaches to seal, more threats to face. If I stop, if I rest, what happens then?"

"Then someone else picks up the burden," Thomas said. "The way you picked it up from your grandmother. The way Aubre will pick it up from you. That's how it works. That's how it's always worked."

Brynn leaned against him, feeling the truth in his words. She'd spent twenty-five years as a guardian—longer than most, given that she should have died in the sealing. She'd done her part. More than her part.

It was time to trust that she'd prepared the next generation well enough to carry on.

That fall, on the twenty-fifth anniversary of the sealing, they gathered at the memorial in the Abyssal Vale—all the survivors of that desperate battle, plus the next generation who'd grown up hearing the stories.

Aubre placed new flowers at the marker. "One hundred and seventy people died here," she said to the assembled crowd. "They bought us a quarter century of peace. Twenty-five years to build, to grow, to prepare for what comes next. That's what sacrifice means. Not the dramatic moment of dying, but what that death enables for those who survive."

Brynn watched her daughter speak and felt pride so intense it was almost painful. Aubre understood. Truly understood. She'd be ready when the crown called her.

That night, alone in her study, Brynn felt the crown pulse with finality.

It's time, it said simply. *I've held the balance as long as I could, but I can't maintain both the seal and you much longer. You need to choose.*

"How long do I have?" Brynn asked.

Weeks. Maybe a month. The seal will hold—I've ensured that. But you... you're fading, Brynn. Your life force is depleting. Soon, there won't be enough left to sustain consciousness.

"And if I choose the seal over my life?"

Then you'll die. Peacefully, painlessly, but permanently. The crown will release you and choose its next guardian. Aubre, most likely.

Brynn sat with that knowledge for a long moment. Twenty-five years. She'd been granted twenty-five years beyond what should have been possible. Twenty-five years to love Thomas, to raise Aubre, to build a legacy.

It was enough.

"I choose the seal," Brynn said clearly. "Maintain it. Don't let it weaken for my sake. I've had more time than I deserved. Let someone else carry the burden now."

As you wish, guardian. You've served well. Better than most. You've earned your rest.

Brynn told Thomas that night, lying in their bed in the small cottage behind the forge. "The crown is failing. I have maybe a month left."

Thomas said nothing for a long moment, just held her. Then: "I'm not ready to lose you."

"No one's ever ready," Brynn said softly. "But I need you to be strong for Aubre. She'll need you after I'm gone."

"I will be. For her. For you."

"Good." Brynn closed her eyes, feeling exhaustion pulling at her. "Thank you, Thomas. For following me. For believing in me. For giving me twenty-five years I shouldn't have had."

"Thank you for letting me follow," Thomas said. "For being someone worth following."

The next month passed in a gentle decline. Brynn grew weaker, slept more, moved less. But she wasn't in pain. The crown kept that away, kept her comfortable as she faded.

Aubre stayed close, learning everything she could in the time that remained. Brynn answered every question, explained every detail, passed on everything she knew about being a guardian.

"The hardest part," Brynn said during one of their last conversations, "isn't the dramatic sacrifices. It's the daily choice to keep going. To carry the burden even when you're tired. That's what breaks most guardians—not the battles but the weight of time."

"How did you endure it?" Aubre asked.

"By remembering I wasn't alone. By accepting help. By understanding that being a guardian doesn't mean being perfect." Brynn smiled weakly. "And by having people I loved waiting for me to come home. Don't forget that, Aubre. Don't let the crown consume you. Keep the human part of yourself alive."

On the last day, Brynn was barely conscious. Thomas sat on one side of her bed, Aubre on the other, holding her hands. Kira stood at the foot, tears streaming down her face. Vera was there too, along with others who'd fought beside Brynn or learned from her.

"It's time," Brynn whispered, feeling the crown preparing to release her. "Take care of each other. Keep the seal strong. Remember what we fought for."

"We will," Aubre promised, her voice breaking. "I promise, Mother. I'll be ready."

"I know," Brynn said. And she did know. She'd prepared her daughter well. The world would be safe.

The crown pulsed one final time, warm and gentle, like a goodbye from an old friend.

Then Brynn Thornwick, guardian of the Crimson Crown, savior of the world, closed her eyes and stopped breathing.

The crown dimmed, then lifted from her head —not falling but floating, moving with purpose. It hung in the air for a moment, considering, judging.

Then it settled onto Aubre's head with a soft light, like starlight captured in metal.

And a new guardian was chosen.

Epilogue

Aubre Thornwick stood in her garden thirty years later, teaching her own daughter about roses and responsibility.

The girl was eight years old, bright and curious, with her grandmother's determination and her mother's steady strength. Aubre had named her Brynn—for the guardian who'd changed everything.

"Your grandmother saved the world," Aubre told little Brynn. "She gave up everything to seal the Shadow Court. But that's not what made her great."

"What did?" young Brynn asked, her eyes wide.

"What made her great was what she did after the dramatic sacrifice. The way she built systems to help future guardians. The way she prepared me to carry on. The way she understood that being a guardian isn't about single moments of glory but about decades of quiet work." Aubre touched the crown that had passed to her thirty years ago. "She taught me that we don't have to save the world alone. That building community, teaching others, creating support networks—that's just as important as sealing breaches."

"Will I have to be a guardian too?" young Brynn asked.

"Maybe," Aubre said honestly. "The crown chooses who it chooses. But if it does choose you, know this—you'll be ready. Because that's what guardians do. We prepare the next generation to be better than we were."

She looked around the garden—roses descended from cuttings her mother had taken from her grandmother's garden, three generations of guardians connected by flowers and duty and love.

Her mother's sacrifice had bought fifty-five years of peace so far. The seal still held strong. The Shadow Court remained imprisoned. The barriers protecting dreamers had been renewed twice under Aubre's watch. The breach network functioned smoothly. The Mage's Guild thrived.

The world was safe.

For now.

For this generation.

And when the next threat came—whether in Aubre's lifetime or young Brynn's or someone else's entirely—there would be guardians ready to face it. Because that's what her mother had built. Not just a seal, but a legacy of preparation, of community, of passing knowledge from one generation to the next.

Aubre heard Thomas—her father, grown old now but still strong—calling from the house. Dinner was ready. The family was gathering.

She took young Brynn's hand and walked toward the house, toward warmth and love and the simple human joys her mother had fought so hard to protect.

The crown rested lightly on her head, a reminder of duty but not a burden. Not anymore. Because she'd learned what her mother had learned: that being a guardian didn't mean standing alone against the darkness.

It meant building a world where light could flourish. Where children could play without fear. Where families could gather for dinner without wondering if tomorrow would come.

That was the legacy.

That was everything.

THE END

A Note To Readers

Thank you for joining Brynn and Thomas on their quest for the Crimson Crown.

If you enjoyed this adventure, I would be deeply grateful if you could take a moment to leave an honest review on Amazon. Reviews help readers discover new stories and support authors in continuing to write the adventures you love.

Even a sentence or two makes a tremendous difference to an independent author.

Thank you for your time, your imagination, and your willingness to believe in magic.

With gratitude,
Jackie L. Smith

Connect With The Author

Enjoyed Brynn Thornwick: Guardian of the Crimson Crown?

Please consider leaving a review on Amazon, Goodreads, or your favorite book platform. Reviews help other readers discover books they might love and support authors in continuing to write stories that matter.

Recommend this book to friends who enjoy:

- Epic fantasy adventures with heart

- Strong friendships and chosen family

- Magical quests and ancient artifacts

- Coming-of-age journeys with courage and wonder

- Stories where ordinary people discover extraordinary destinies

Stay Connected:

Twitter/X: @CheckerBoa81267

Facebook: jacksmith1591

Thank you for reading Brynn Thornwick, Guardian of the Crimson Crown. Your support means everything to an author pursuing the dream of storytelling.

May you always chase your own crimson crowns.

— Jackie L. Smith

Acknowledgments

This book would not exist without the support of grandchildren, nieces and nephews, and other people who believed in magic and encouraged me to write it down.

To my family—thank you for understanding when I disappeared into fantasy worlds and emerged hours later with stories to tell. Your patience with my creative obsessions made this possible.

To my early readers—your feedback, encouragement, and honest critiques shaped this story into something worthy of sharing with the world. Every "what happens next?" kept me writing.

To the teachers, librarians, and storytellers who fostered my love of fantasy—you planted seeds that grew into entire worlds. Thank you for showing me that magic exists in the pages of books.

To readers everywhere who still believe in quests, crowns, and the power of friendship—this story is for you. May you always find adventures worth taking.

And to anyone who's ever felt ordinary but suspected they might be destined for something extraordinary—you are. Keep searching for your crown.

About The Author

Jackie L. Smith has always believed in the magic hidden just beyond the edges of the everyday world. As a child, he used to play in caves back in the hills of Kentucky, playing pirates and cowboys and Indians with his brothers. They truly believed in magic at that young age and loved adventures, seeking to find one every day they were out of school.

Brynn Thornwick: Guardian of the Crimson Crown is his third novel, a story born from a lifetime love of fantasy adventures, ancient maps, and the belief that courage lives in ordinary people who dare to chase impossible dreams.

When not writing about magical quests, Jackie enjoys reading, fishing, cooking, and the occasional game of FreeCell.

He currently resides with his family in Staffordsville, Kentucky.